Unintended Consequences

by

Jann Rowland

One Good Sonnet Publishing
Publishers of Fine Romance
and Fantasy Fiction

By Jann Rowland

Published by One Good Sonnet Publishing:

PRIDE AND PREJUDICE VARIATIONS

Unintended Consequences
More Agreeably Engaged
Bonds of Love
Danger at the Netherfield Ball
No Cause to Repine
Among Intimate Acquaintances
In Default of Heirs Male
Prisoner of Longbourn
Bonds of Friendship
Quitting the Sphere

UNINTENDED CONSEQUENCES

Copyright © 2022 Jann Rowland

Cover Design by Jann Rowland

Published by One Good Sonnet Publishing

ISBN: 1-989212-90-5
ISBN-13: 978-1-989212-90-5

To my family who have, as always, shown
their unconditional love and encouragement.

CHAPTER I

"'*D*epend upon it, sir, when a man knows he is to be hanged in a fortnight, it concentrates his mind wonderfully.'"

"Darcy," said Fitzwilliam, piercing his introspection, "did you just compare marrying Cousin Anne with being condemned to the gallows?" Fitzwilliam paused and grinned and then added: "Samuel Johnson, is it not?"

"It is," murmured Darcy, still standing at the window and gazing out on the street below.

Two days before, he had been at Rosings Park, enduring his Aunt Catherine's ways and trying to fend off her continual efforts to induce him to marry Anne. Two days before, he had been unexpectedly enjoying his sojourn in Kent, all because of the presence of a visitor to the parsonage.

Darcy scowled down at the street outside his window. It was precisely because of his aunt that he was now in London, the season still ongoing in the city, not that Darcy could muster any interest in it. Not with his aunt's latest machinations to force him to the altar still ringing in his mind. It was for that reason he was no longer enjoying Miss Elizabeth's company.

Everything had been proceeding well, as far as Darcy had been concerned. Lady Catherine was, as always, difficult to endure, and there was not much to do at Rosings other than look through her books and ride the estate. Darcy had been contemplating his future, and more particularly, whether he could safely put aside his objections to Miss Elizabeth's condition in life and offer for her. He had all but surrendered, if Darcy was honest, though at the time he had not confessed that he had lost the battle with his inner self to remain impervious to her charms.

All that changed Thursday evening, and not for the better. The day had been fine, and Fitzwilliam had noted upon returning to the house that he had met Miss Elizabeth while touring the park. His cousin's words had surprised Darcy, though he had also been relieved he would not need to contend for her attention if he decided to proceed.

"She is a lovely woman, Cousin," said Fitzwilliam after speaking of meeting her in the woods surrounding Rosings. "I know not if you plan to make her an offer but you could do far worse than Miss Elizabeth. And you should not allow Lady Catherine's displeasure to prevent you."

"Do you suppose I would?" Darcy had asked, not bothering to deny his interest; they had spoken of Miss Elizabeth enough that his cousin knew of Darcy's fascination for her.

"No, I do not suppose it." Fitzwilliam put his foot on the edge of the table in the library, an action that would bring Lady Catherine's condemnation if she witnessed it. "But I do not know your mind yet, as you have not seen fit to share. All the admiration in the world will serve you nothing if you do not act."

"That is the truth," replied Darcy. "But what of Miss Bennet's situation in life? My father married the daughter of an earl; should I not set my sights on a similar match?"

"Your father married your mother because he was besotted with her," said Fitzwilliam with a snort. "And by all accounts, he equally affected your mother. Besides, have you not always droned on about how the history of your family contains many ladies who would not have been acceptable by society's standards?"

"That is true," replied Darcy. He paused and eyed his cousin. "Did she seem happy today?"

"As she usually is." Fitzwilliam scratched at his chin for a moment, then shrugged. "After we had walked for some time, she claimed a headache, requiring me to escort her back to the parsonage. I would have, regardless, but she truly appeared in some distress."

Darcy's heart clenched painfully in his breast. Was he so far gone in love that he could not bear the thought of her experiencing any pain? Any attempt to wrap her in cotton to protect her would bring out Miss Elizabeth's fiery temper, he was certain, even if such a thing were possible.

"Perhaps I should visit the parsonage to inquire after her," mused Darcy.

"Are the parson and his family not to come to Rosings tonight?"

"And we will all be under Lady Catherine's watchful eye. That is not a comfortable place to make love to a woman."

Fitzwilliam snorted. "Perhaps it is not. Then you should arrange to meet her on one of the paths of the estate. That would afford you more privacy."

"In saying as much, you presuppose I have not already done so."

What tease Fitzwilliam might have offered remained unspoken, for, at that moment, the door opened, and in strode a whirlwind in silks and lace. As was her custom, Lady Catherine's dress might have been appropriate for a ball in Almack's, or a dinner with a duchess. Thus she always was, for she had no head for economy and an aristocrat's notion of keeping the distinction of rank.

"Darcy," greeted she, her manner as offensive as it usually was. "I have looked everywhere for you."

"Oh?" asked Darcy, only mildly interested. He had noticed that Fitzwilliam removed his foot from the table as soon as the door opened, a fact which was far more diverting than anything Lady Catherine might have said.

"Yes, for I have something which I would say to you."

Inwardly, Darcy sighed, for he was certain he knew what this presaged. But he had no time to reply, for Lady Catherine continued at once.

"As you know, I have hoped this would be the year you would stop dithering and come to the point with Anne. I tire of waiting, so I will ask you one more time—when do you mean to ask for her hand?"

"I do not mean to ask for her hand, Aunt," replied Darcy quietly.

Perhaps it was for the best, after all. While he had avoided the subject and done all he could to provoke Lady Catherine to drop her insistence, he had rarely spoken openly for fear of inciting an argument. If he was to pursue Miss Elizabeth, surely it would be better to disabuse his aunt now, allow her anger to cool for a time, then present her new niece when she had regained her equilibrium. Any hope of acceptance was likely fantasy, but Darcy indulged in it, nevertheless.

"Nothing binds me to Anne," said Darcy, these thoughts passing through his mind in an instant. "You speak of my mother's wishes, but she mentioned nothing of an engagement to Anne, and my father openly disparaged the very notion. Please, Lady Catherine, drop the subject. I do not wish to marry Anne, and she does not wish to marry me."

"Anne will do as she is told," snapped Lady Catherine, the light of anger already burning in her eyes.

"But I will not," replied Darcy, keeping his temper firmly in check. "All you will accomplish by pursuing this is a break in the family. Desist, I beg of you."

Lady Catherine watched him through narrowed eyes. "It is unfortunate that you have proved recalcitrant, for it rouses me to actions I would prefer to avoid contemplating. I shall assume your obstinacy has nothing to do with the distraction which recently appeared in our midst, for your rebellion predates her coming by many years. And I have it on good authority that you remember yourself enough to refrain from pursuing unsuitable women."

What the devil was his aunt saying? Surely, she could not suspect his interest in Miss Elizabeth, for he had been entirely careful to practice circumspection in her company, knowing what her reaction would be. No, the mere presence of a pretty young woman was enough to rouse her suspicions, and in this instance, she had already cast the notion aside without plying him with her brand of insistence.

"Whatever is prompting it, your defiance must stop." His aunt's voice was firm and immovable as Rosings itself. "You *will* marry Anne as you were intended."

"I have already said I will not."

"Perhaps you have. But you do not understand the hold I have over you. You will marry my daughter, or you will suffer the consequences."

Darcy regarded her, wondering what the virago was saying. "I know of no such hold, Lady Catherine. I am my own man. Pemberley is mine and my fortune is free of encumbrance. If you possess such a means to compel me, I invite you to inform me of what it is."

His aunt stood tall and proud, her bearing betraying no doubt, the confidence emanating out from her in waves. "What of your sister's little adventure this past summer?"

For a moment, Darcy did not understand to what his aunt referred. Then a surge of anger exploded within him, and he took an involuntary step, putting himself directly in front of her. From his position on the sofa, Darcy could hear Fitzwilliam's hissed inhalation and heard him jump to his feet, heard his menacing stride approaching.

"Of what are you speaking?" demanded Darcy.

"Do not obfuscate, insolent boy! Your reaction has all but confirmed my information as nothing but the truth."

"And where did you receive this intelligence?" pressed Darcy. "What do you know?"

"My source and extent of my knowledge I shall keep to myself," said Lady Catherine, her step to the side smooth, as if she were merely walking while thinking, rather than taking herself from his intimidating presence. "But I know enough to apprehend that if this information was disseminated to the public, it would be ruinous."

"You would hurt your niece to force Darcy?" queried Fitzwilliam, his voice as low and dangerous as Darcy knew his own to be. "What kind of woman would do such a thing?"

"Blame Darcy!" spat Lady Catherine, whirling on Fitzwilliam, one bony finger extended. "If he would do his duty and propose to my daughter, I would not need to resort to such threats."

"You are bluffing," declared Darcy. "You would never open Georgiana to such infamy for no other reason than your selfish concerns. And what would the earl say?"

"I care little for my brother," said Lady Catherine. "This is between the Darcys and the de Bourghs—the Fitzwilliams are not involved." Lady Catherine turned to Fitzwilliam and waved him away. "You may leave, Nephew, for your opinion is neither wanted nor is this a matter that concerns you."

"Fustian nonsense!" snarled Fitzwilliam. "You propose to ruin my ward; that makes it my concern."

Lady Catherine ground her teeth together but ignored Fitzwilliam in favor of Darcy. "Do you truly wish to test my resolve?"

"Do you truly propose to hurt my sister for no other reason than your own selfish desires?"

The lady's gaze bored into Darcy, not a shred of give in her manner. "You will march into the sitting-room where my daughter awaits, and there you will propose to her. If you do not, you will not like the consequences."

"In that case, Lady Catherine," replied Darcy, clenching and unclenching his fists to avoid throttling her, "I shall not stay another minute in this house. You may consider all connection between the Darcys and the de Bourghs hereby severed."

As Darcy stalked from the room, he called for his carriage and his valet, instructing Snell to gather his things and follow him to London in the second carriage. His aunt's continual harangue, he ignored. He said he would not stay another instant in that house, and he meant it.

"You took a chance walking out on her as you did."

Fitzwilliam's voice pulled Darcy from his dark memories, prompting him to turn and regard his cousin. "I do not believe I did. Even Lady Catherine is not so selfish as to lack understanding about what her brother would say if she even breathed a hint of what she knows of last summer. I knew even then that Lady Catherine would settle on browbeating me through letters for a time. I am still uncertain she is not bluffing entirely."

"There is one problem with your assertion, Darcy," said Fitzwilliam. "You presume that Lady Catherine is sensible. Do not make the mistake of supposing she will hold back. Everything, our ties as family, her affection for Georgiana, even the need to keep our family from the tongues of the gossips—all these things pale in comparison with her lust to connect her line with Pemberley." Fitzwilliam paused and shook his head. "My father has suggested more than once she wished to have your father for herself. She has always burned with jealousy of your mother for catching the prize she could not."

"And now she means to have Pemberley through her daughter."

"Exactly."

Darcy gave his cousin a dark grin. "She should take care for what she wishes. If she succeeds in this mad design, *I* shall own Rosings. She would not appreciate her situation if I owned the estate she calls home."

"She does not care and will not listen," said Fitzwilliam, shaking his head. "Even if you threatened her with it, I doubt she would consider it seriously."

"When does your father return?"

Fitzwilliam shook his head and leaned back in his chair. "I have sent him an express, as you know. But it will be a fortnight before he receives it. The problem at the Ireland estate was so severe that it even caused his absence while parliament is in session. I doubt he will come in time to control her."

Darcy grimaced, for his conclusion had been the same. "Your father might have supported her anyway, considering what he said at the end of last season of my need to marry."

"I doubt it," replied Fitzwilliam. "My father wishes to see the succession at Pemberley confirmed, but not at the expense of marrying you to Anne. He understands her limitations and knows she is not what you need in a wife."

"And would he accept a woman of little prominence and dowry?"

Fitzwilliam regarded him, betraying no hint of his feelings. "You speak of Miss Elizabeth."

"Perhaps," replied Darcy. "Do you think your father would accept her?"

"You know him as well as I do." Fitzwilliam shrugged and continued: "I suspect he will not exactly be pleased, but I doubt he would do anything other than welcome her into the family, for he will not wish for any gossip to stain us. Now, please explain what you are thinking, Darcy, for I am having trouble following you."

"Just this: if I am already married, Lady Catherine will have no hold over me, for I cannot marry *two* women."

"And you suppose she will not publish Georgiana's misstep in retaliation for defying her?"

"I cannot predict what she will do," replied Darcy. "But I cannot marry Anne, and this is a plan that is as likely to work as any other we have discussed."

"I do not know, Darcy."

As a matter of fact, Darcy did not know himself. But Anne was sickly and small, and Darcy did not know if she possessed the ability to serve as Pemberley's mistress, to say nothing about whether the strength required to bear him an heir was in her grasp. If he could not marry Anne, the next best option was to remove the possibility altogether, thereby removing Lady Catherine's leverage. She may still be vindictive enough to proceed regardless of what he did, but Darcy thought there was a better chance of persuading her to desist, though he knew this was likely the end of all congress between the Darcy and de Bourgh branches of the family. Darcy thought he could endure a permanent estrangement with great cheer.

"'Integrity without knowledge is weak and useless, and knowledge without integrity is dangerous and dreadful,'" murmured Darcy without thinking.

Fitzwilliam eyed him. "Johnson again?"

"It is," confirmed Darcy. "You must own that it fits this situation, and Lady Catherine, in particular, very well."

"It does," agreed Fitzwilliam. He paused for a moment, considering, and then said: "How do you suppose Lady Catherine learned of Ramsgate?"

"There were only a few who knew of it," said Darcy, counting off the names as he spoke. "You and I, Georgiana herself, your parents, and a few servants, all of whom I trust implicitly. And two others: George Wickham and Sarah Younge."

Fitzwilliam understood the implications at once, as evidenced by his scowl. "Mrs. Younge was rather intimidated by it all, as I recall."

"She was," replied Darcy. "I would not expect her to even know that approaching Aunt Catherine might be profitable, though it may be better to tie up that loose end and nullify her ability to spread rumors. Wickham, however, is another matter. He would do anything to gain a copper."

"And he knows Lady Catherine and knows she would jump at the chance to gain leverage that might force you to the altar. I suppose I must begin a search for our friend. Whatever you say, I mean to ensure he is never in a position to hurt our family again."

"Ah, but you do not know what I know," replied Darcy, feeling a dark smugness well up within him. "Not only do I know where to find Wickham, but I would not stop you even if you meant to beat him to death with the flat of your cavalry saber. Even if my conjecture is untrue, he has caused enough harm to my family to deserve double the retribution I mean to bring upon his head."

Fitzwilliam gave him an evil grin. "Do tell, Darcy. I have a great desire to see our old friend again."

They discussed the matter, Fitzwilliam expressing surprise that Darcy had known of Wickham's whereabouts since the previous autumn. At length, when they had decided on the details of George Wickham's apprehension and fate, Fitzwilliam sat back and considered Darcy.

"Do you suppose Miss Elizabeth's sojourn to Kent put the notion of Lady Catherine into Wickham's head?"

Darcy shrugged. "It is possible, though I cannot be certain."

Fitzwilliam nodded. "Then we return to the other subject we discussed. Do you truly mean to thumb your nose at Lady Catherine and offer for Miss Elizabeth?"

"I do," said Darcy. "She is an excellent and capable woman and would do well as my wife." A part of Darcy whispered in his ear that he was also besotted with her, but Darcy ignored the voice. There would be enough time to make his feelings clear after they were married. At present, time was of the essence.

"I am not certain that is at all wise. There were several times in her company that I did not think she particularly liked you."

"Pardon me, Fitzwilliam, but I have no notion of what you are saying. She does not like me?"

"It is her combativity when in your company," said Fitzwilliam. "What of her expectation that you had said nothing good of her? What of her comments at the pianoforte at Rosings? I have often had the impression that her repartee to you was harder, not in keeping with her usual playful manner of speaking with others."

"I have seen nothing of it," said Darcy with a frown.

Fitzwilliam shook his head, indicating his capitulation. "Perhaps I am reading too much into her behavior. You *are* better acquainted with her than I, after all. How do you mean to do it? You cannot return to Rosings."

"She is to return home soon," said Darcy. "Next week, if I am not mistaken. The estate Bingley leased is quite near her father's home. I believe I can prevail upon Bingley to return thither, though I hesitate to return him to that place. Then I will be near enough to pay court to her at my leisure." Darcy paused and gave his cousin a rueful grin. "Or at least as much leisure as Aunt Catherine will allow."

The nod with which Fitzwilliam responded soon gave way to shock and a sickly expression. "Bingley? Was he the one you recently saved from a most imprudent marriage?"

"I would not say that, exactly." Darcy felt his lips contort. "I assisted his sisters to point out the drawbacks to an alliance with a young lady of the neighborhood, but I would not take all the credit. Returning to Netherfield will put Bingley in the lady's proximity again, but I suppose it cannot be helped."

"This lady," said Fitzwilliam, his manner earnest. "Is she known to Miss Elizabeth?"

Uncertain and feeling dread well up within him, Darcy nodded. "It is Miss Elizabeth's sister."

Fitzwilliam groaned and rested his head in his hand. "I am sorry, Darcy, for I did not know. That must be why Miss Elizabeth became ill; she must have feigned it. Now that I think about it, her response was a little off. At the time, however, I was not looking for it and did not realize."

"What the devil are you saying?" demanded Darcy.

"When I met Miss Elizabeth in the park," replied Fitzwilliam, his countenance ashen. "The subject of you and Bingley arose, though I do not recall how, and I made some mention of how you had lately saved a friend from an imprudent marriage."

Darcy felt an icy fist clench his heart. "I declare, Fitzwilliam," said he, though lacking heat, "sometimes you gossip worse than an old woman!" The lack of anger was an acknowledgment to himself that the situation was his fault and no other.

"I had no idea it would be anything other than an amusing anecdote." When Darcy glared at him, Fitzwilliam chuckled and held out his hand. "I know—I should not have been so eager to share it."

With a nod, Darcy passed a weary hand over his face. "Then my suit is not so certain as I had thought."

"If you considered it certain, I must question your judgment." Darcy looked to his cousin, who was not hesitant to explain. "If there is any woman who would think nothing of your fortune or situation in life, I declare that woman is Miss Elizabeth Bennet. I have never met someone so little likely to be impressed by such things."

The comment struck Darcy as apropos.

"Besides, have you not always complained of ladies who see you for nothing more than your pocketbook? Had you not cocked it up, I might have thought Miss Elizabeth was the perfect woman for you. Not that it matters now, I suppose."

"The situation might still be salvageable," said Darcy, a hint of an idea coming to him.

Fitzwilliam regarded him with interest, but Darcy's concentration was now all inward. His cousin's comment about Miss Elizabeth's integrity had jarred something else loose, something he had not considered.

"What do you mean?" asked Fitzwilliam, after a few moments.

"Just what you said about how my position would not impress her," replied Darcy. "You are completely correct, of course—Miss Elizabeth is not a fortune hunter." Darcy grimaced and regarded his cousin, saying: "Her mother, on the other hand, is the most blatant fortune hunter I have ever met."

"Do you suppose her mother can influence her?"

"No, I do not suppose it. In fact, I had the distinct impression that Mr. Collins fixed his attention on *her* at Bingley's ball. It surprised me to learn that Miss Elizabeth was visiting Kent as a *guest* of her friend, Mrs. Collins."

"*That* is a hideous thought," said Fitzwilliam, giving a theatrical shudder. "To think of a woman such as Miss Elizabeth Bennet married to a toad like Collins is beyond consideration."

"I agree with you," said Darcy, reflecting on how relieved he had been to learn Mrs. Collins and Miss Elizabeth were not one and the same. "While I cannot guess what diverted his attention, it strikes me that she would not marry for material gain—William Collins, or me if it came to that."

"Then where does that leave you?"

"Perhaps in a better position than I had thought. I must give her other reasons to consider me as a prospective husband."

"There is still the matter of her elder sister and Bingley."

"That is perhaps the easiest to deal with," replied Darcy. "After all, I will need Bingley's assistance when I return to Hertfordshire. As Bingley and Miss Bennet are both in London, it would be a simple matter to inform Bingley of her presence."

Darcy paused to consider it and then grimaced. "Or perhaps it will not be so simple, for Bingley is likely to be angry at my interference."

"How did it come about?"

"Miss Bingley was wild to prevent a union between them, for she does not consider Miss Bennet high enough for her brother."

Fitzwilliam snorted his disdain. "No doubt she considers herself akin to a duchess."

"I shall not say you are incorrect. For my part, I had watched Miss Bennet at Bingley's ball and other locations, and I could not see any hint of peculiar regard on her part. But it seems I must revise my opinion—Miss Elizabeth is unhappy about my actions there, and I doubt she would be so offended if her sister had not been injured. Now I must wonder if I was mistaken."

For a long moment, his cousin regarded him. "A lady such as Miss Elizabeth would leave a man in no doubt of her regard if she espoused such feelings."

"That is where you are incorrect," said Darcy. "Miss Bennet is reticent, perhaps as much as I am myself."

"Then your path seems clear. If you reunite them, that will remove a large part of her resentment against you. With that put to rest, perhaps you can persuade her."

Later, after his cousin had gone, Darcy considered the situation and tried to think of it without the light of prejudice shining in his eyes. While the notion of putting Bingley in Miss Bennet's sights again had concerned him, this new information about the potential mistake he had made in warning his friend from her would right a wrong he had not even known he had committed. Yes, Bingley might be angry with him, but it was a small price to pay, and he knew his friend was not the resentful sort.

And it would not do him any harm in Miss Elizabeth's eyes. Quite the contrary, in fact.

CHAPTER II

"*I*s something wrong, Lizzy?"

Elizabeth Bennet looked up from the letter that had so shocked her, meeting the concerned eyes of her close friend. Mr. Collins, she noted, was also watching her, as was Mariah. Was that a look of eagerness in the parson's eyes, the hope that her letter contained bad news about her father, leading to his inheritance? Elizabeth shook off such thoughts, for she could not imagine even such a silly man as William Collins rejoicing in the misfortune of her family, even if it would be to his benefit.

"No, Charlotte, nothing is amiss," replied Elizabeth, looking back down at her letter. "It is only that Jane's letter has astonished me exceedingly."

Charlotte's expression demanded an explanation, and Elizabeth did not hesitate to give it, regardless of how she could scarce comprehend it. "Jane writes that she has seen Mr. Bingley in London."

"Has she?" said Charlotte, her interest plain. "That is surprising for did you not say it was unlikely she would see him again?"

"Given Miss Bingley's behavior when Jane last saw her, I cannot account for it." Elizabeth paused and skimmed Jane's letter, which was shorter than was her sister's wont and written in a perturbation of spirit. "Jane makes no mention of how it came about—she only says that Mr. Bingley visited her at Uncle's house on Gracechurch Street. She does not even say much of his behavior, though if I read between the lines, I suspect his eagerness has not diminished in the intervening months."

"That is truly fortunate for your excellent sister," said Mr. Collins, nodding in Elizabeth's direction. "My Charlotte has informed me of how much Miss Bennet has suffered. Perhaps this will work to the benefit of your family, for I cannot help but suppose an alliance to Mr. Bingley—and through him, a connection to Mr. Darcy—would improve your position."

Elizabeth eyed the parson, suspecting he was concerned for their futures and the possibility he might be called upon to support them. A look from Charlotte caught Elizabeth's eye, and a slight shake of her head told her it would be best to refrain from trading words with him. As such, she offered a banal reply, which appeared to satisfy him, and turned her attention back to her breakfast. He did not spare her of his need to pontificate, but Elizabeth ignored him, much the same as she had every other occasion she had been in his company since coming to Kent. Mr. Collins did not notice her incivility.

That did not mean there was no further conversation on the subject. Charlotte, Elizabeth knew, esteemed Jane as much as she did herself, and she would wish to know more. Thus, when Mr. Collins went to his study, Charlotte drew Elizabeth to her parlor for further discussion.

"This matter of Jane and Mr. Bingley is surprising, Lizzy," said Charlotte when they were situated therein. "How do you suppose it came about?"

"I cannot say, for Jane says nothing of the particulars." With a rueful look at her friend, Elizabeth said: "Perhaps Mr. Darcy became ashamed with his actions in separating them and left early to inform Mr. Bingley of his mistake."

Charlotte shook her head with fondness. "I know that you hardly suppose Mr. Darcy was the means of reuniting them. Besides, while the gentlemen left unexpectedly on Thursday, they were here longer than they usually stay. I have heard they delayed their departure at least twice."

"Perhaps they find Lady Catherine's company curiously agreeable," replied Elizabeth impishly. "But you are correct—Mr. Darcy cannot have told Mr. Bingley of Jane's presence. I can only assume Mr. Bingley discovered it through his sister, though I suppose a chance meeting is not beyond possibility."

"Now I must think you are mad, Elizabeth. Do you suppose that Miss Bingley would inform her brother whereas Mr. Darcy doing the same is impossible?"

Elizabeth laughed and shook her head. "No, but a chance comment exposing the matter, or some other means of his learning of it seems the likeliest."

"Then I suppose there is nothing to do but wait to receive Jane's account of it."

"And for that, I must wait another five days, for I do not suppose Jane will write again before I depart."

Elizabeth felt an eagerness to return to London well up within her, but she would not show as much to her friend. Thus, for her remaining days, she made every attempt to present a contented front, and despite her eagerness to learn what was happening between Jane and Mr. Bingley, she found solace in Charlotte's company, knowing their separation, when it came again, might be of some duration.

They continued in this manner the final few days of her stay there, much as they had before Mr. Darcy's arrival. The one major difference was the lack of any notice from Rosings, for since Mr. Darcy had departed, Lady Catherine had not invited them to her home, and other than Sunday at church, where she had returned to her home as soon as the service ended, they saw nothing of the lady or her daughter. The speculation of why she had canceled their engagement the night Mr. Darcy had departed remained a subject between them, but they could not say the reason for it, as Lady Catherine remained silent.

Mr. Collins was not, of course, sanguine about his lack of society with his patroness, as he made known several times a day. Her ladyship, he reported, had seemed out of spirits since her nephews' departure, and Lady Catherine's servants had met his entreaties to see her with a firm declaration that she did not wish to be disturbed. The longer this went on, the more despondent the parson became.

This all changed the day before Elizabeth was to depart from Kent. That morning, Elizabeth had spent her time preparing her effects for the morrow, and in this Charlotte, who appeared unwilling to be parted from her any longer than she must, joined her. They also included Maria in this, though the girl appeared to view the return journey to Hertfordshire as a lark, completely missing the point of how she would be separated from her sister. She was not callous, Elizabeth knew—she was young and enthusiastic about everything and was not yet accustomed to seeing anything other than her foremost interest.

After they had completed these tasks, the three ladies ensconced themselves in the parlor for one last afternoon in each other's company. While they were in this attitude, the murmur of voices began beyond the door, the masculine tones of Mr. Collins along with a female voice of such volume that the ladies knew at once who it was.

". . . honored by your visit to our humble abode, Lady Catherine," came the voice of Mr. Collins as the door opened, the parson escorting her ladyship into the room amid bows low enough for an empress. "Charlotte and I are, as always, gratified by your attention and eager to hear whatever words of wisdom you see it to impart, for it is always excellent advice that one cannot help but follow to the letter!"

As she stepped into the room, Lady Catherine regarded the three ladies there, who had risen at her coming. What her scrutiny might portend Elizabeth could not say, but she had the distinct impression that Lady Catherine's gaze had rested longer on her than on her two companions. Her ladyship's first words removed any doubt in Elizabeth's mind that she was correct.

"Mrs. Collins," said she with a slight nod of her head, "I should like to speak to your young friend for a few moments." Her eyes then found Elizabeth again. "If you will oblige me, Miss Elizabeth."

"You wish to speak to my cousin?" asked Mr. Collins with more surprise than sense. "Has she offended you, Lady Catherine? If so, I apologize with the utmost sincerity and assure you—"

"There is nothing about which you need concern yourself, Mr. Collins," snapped Lady Catherine, bringing him up short. "It is nothing more than a desire to ask her opinion. Mrs. Collins, I shall have need of this room."

Charlotte paused and looked at Elizabeth. As it happened, Elizabeth was not opposed to speaking with Lady Catherine and knew nothing of why the lady might be angry with her. She could not, at the same time, think of anything with which she might assist Lady Catherine, but Elizabeth did not suppose she would take being denied with any grace. Thus, she gave Charlotte a nod of assent.

"Come, Mr. Collins, Maria," said Charlotte, her practical nature coming to the fore. "Let us leave Lady Catherine and Elizabeth alone."

It was clear Mr. Collins was not eager to depart, but he allowed Charlotte to guide him from the room. He cast one last look over his shoulder in supplication. Elizabeth could not imagine she would anger Lady Catherine, but she smiled at him, which seemed to ease him a little.

When the door closed behind them, Lady Catherine motioned to the sofa where Elizabeth had been sitting before her arrival. "Let us sit, Miss Elizabeth. There is no need to concern yourself."

"I never would have thought there was," replied Elizabeth calmly as she sat. "How may I assist?"

Lady Catherine chose a nearby chair, and for a long moment, she regarded Elizabeth, as if attempting to see through to her. What that could be about, Elizabeth could not say, but she maintained her composure and waited for her ladyship to state her reason for this interview.

"I wish to ask you concerning my nephew, Miss Elizabeth. Mr. Darcy, to be precise."

Curiosity raged through Elizabeth as she said: "About Mr. Darcy? I do not understand."

The lady considered her words. "Might I assume you know something of my daughter's engagement to my nephew?"

"I have heard something of it," replied Elizabeth cautiously. "But I do not know the details."

"That is not germane to the subject at hand."

Lady Catherine's hard gaze seemed to dare Elizabeth to disagree; Elizabeth had no thought to do so, contenting herself, instead, with waiting for Lady Catherine to continue to speak.

"Suffice it to say that their engagement is a long-acknowledged fact, and my sister and I spoke of it while they were both very young."

Privately, Elizabeth thought any expectation Lady Catherine had of Mr. Darcy marrying her daughter was naïve at best. While she could say nothing of the legalities and whether there was a contract, her observation had informed her that Mr. Darcy possessed no affinity for Miss de Bourgh. Given their ages, if he intended to offer for her, Elizabeth was certain he would have done it already. Mr. Darcy had never struck her as a man inclined to be browbeaten, and something of Lady Catherine's application spoke to his recalcitrance.

"Thus," continued the lady, "I suspect you can understand why I would be jealous of any indication there may be an impediment to my designs."

"Yes, I can," replied Elizabeth, though she thought this was a clearer testament of Mr. Darcy's lack of willingness to follow his aunt's dictates. "What I cannot understand is what this has to do with me."

"Nothing, I hope. You are a pretty young woman, Miss Elizabeth, one who may possess the necessary attributes to turn my nephew's attention away from his duty. It is clear Fitzwilliam finds you agreeable, though my observations of Darcy have been inconclusive."

"You suspect *me* of attempting to draw your nephew in?" asked Elizabeth, aware the conversation may deteriorate if she did not give Lady Catherine the assurance she required.

The lady again fell silent for a moment, regarding her, before saying: "No, I do not suppose it of you. Regardless of your unfortunate tendency to speak more decidedly than you ought, I have never thought you insensible of your own good."

"Then why are we having this discussion?" asked Elizabeth, confused.

"Because I find myself uncertain of my nephew, even if I am confident of my assessment of you."

"Indeed?" asked Elizabeth. "Then you believe Mr. Darcy has made overtures to me?"

"Has he?" demanded the lady.

For a moment, Elizabeth thought to inform the lady exactly what she thought of Mr. Darcy, reassuring her of the utter impossibility of what she suggested. Discretion, however, rescued her from making such a mistake, for she did not think Lady Catherine would appreciate hearing Elizabeth disparage her nephew, any more than she would wish to hear that they were already engaged.

"Then let me put your mind at ease," said Elizabeth, eager to end this interview. "Mr. Darcy has made no overtures of any kind to me, not in all the time I have known him. Furthermore, I cannot imagine that he would ever offer the kind of interest in me that you are suggesting. While I have no notion of his feelings regarding his engagement, there has never been any hint of any interest in me that would prevent his union with your daughter. I would never presume to push myself between them or frustrate your designs."

Lady Catherine let out an explosive breath, and for the first time, Elizabeth thought she caught a hint of a smile from the lady. "That is well. I thank you for alleviating my concerns in so forthright a manner, for I would not have wished to pull the truth from you had you vacillated."

"That is why I responded the way I did," replied Elizabeth. "I do not wish to earn your disapprobation, Lady Catherine, and I have nothing to hide."

"Very well," said Lady Catherine. "Then it should be no trouble for you to give me your solemn promise that you will never accept any sort of proposal from my nephew should he lose himself enough to offer it."

Again, Elizabeth found herself shocked. "Do you think he may?"

"As I said," replied Lady Catherine, "you are a young woman, impertinent and confident enough to provide a lure for my nephew, and not lacking in beauty. I believe you when you say you do not expect any overtures from him and do not seek them, but I believe my nephew could develop an interest in you regardless of your determination."

"That is extraordinary, Lady Catherine!" exclaimed Elizabeth. "For Mr. Darcy has given no hint of it, nor can I believe he ever would."

"And yet I would have your promise."

"It is unnecessary," replied Elizabeth. "I cannot imagine he would ever approach me with such intentions in mind, and I find it equally difficult to believe I would accept him if he should."

Lady Catherine gazed at her for several long moments. Then she nodded, slowly at first, and with increasing confidence a moment later.

"Then I believe that is what I require. I thank you for your indulgence and wish you a pleasant journey to your home. It was my intention to invite you to Rosings on the last day of your stay here, but I am not at liberty to do so at present. I hope you understand."

"Of course, Lady Catherine," said Elizabeth, rising with her ladyship. "Please do not suppose I am offended, for you have been the soul of hospitality during my stay, and I thank you for your attention."

With a regal nod, the Lady Catherine departed the room. Elizabeth sank back into her seat, wondering at what had just taken place, paying little heed to the voices that reached her ears from beyond the door. More of Lady Catherine's ubiquitous instructions, she had no doubt. That Lady Catherine had thought Mr. Darcy capable of fixing his attentions on the humble Miss Elizabeth Bennet of Longbourn in Hertfordshire was astonishing. That she had thought enough of it to demand a promise to refuse him if he should propose was beyond belief.

"Cousin Elizabeth!"

Mr. Collins hurried into the room, Charlotte and Maria following, telling Elizabeth that Lady Catherine had finally departed. The way the parson regarded her, his wild eyes showing the whites, the wringing of his hands, suggested she had not calmed him before she left.

"Did you offend Lady Catherine?"

"No, Mr. Collins," said Elizabeth, pushing her confusion to the side. "Did she appear displeased?"

That brought the parson up short.

"Not at all," said Charlotte into the silence. "Had she been angry with Elizabeth, you know she would have said something on the subject."

"Yes, I suppose she would have," mused Mr. Collins. "Then about what did she wish to speak to you?"

"My apologies, Mr. Collins, but it is a private matter between Lady Catherine and me. It has been resolved satisfactorily and there is no need to fear her anger."

Elizabeth feared the parson might demand an answer, but it appeared he thought better of it. It was more likely his hesitance was about what Lady Catherine would think of his demands if news of it ever made its way back to her. It was fortunate for Elizabeth's peace of mind that he murmured a few words of understanding and took himself from the room.

"Oh, Lizzy!" exclaimed Maria when he was gone. "I am happy Lady Catherine wished to speak with *you*, for I would have been too petrified for words!"

"Lady Catherine is not so fearsome, Maria," replied Elizabeth with a warm smile for the girl. "In fact, I believe she respects confidence."

Maria did not appear to know what to say, and Charlotte stepped into the breach. "Lizzy is correct, Maria. Now, have you completed your preparations for the morrow?"

"I shall return to my room and ensure everything is ready," said Maria. "For before she left, Lady Catherine asked after my packing and told me the proper way to arrange my dresses and avoid wrinkles. If I am to finish before dinner, I had best get to it!"

So saying, the girl departed from the room, her footsteps on the stairs a testament to her hurry to put Lady Catherine's advice into practice. Charlotte turned to face Elizabeth, and Elizabeth could not help but feel the mirth bubble up within her. Her friend's next act was to go to the door and close it before she returned to Elizabeth for the inevitable inquisition.

"While you may have put my husband and sister off, Lizzy, I am more discerning than they. Lady Catherine does not appear angry with you; I also doubt this is a matter you must hold in confidence. Shall you not share it with me?"

"I hardly know what to make of it myself," replied Elizabeth with a shake of her head.

"Then tell me, so that I may help decipher whatever Lady Catherine told you."

Elizabeth laughed. "It seems Lady Catherine suspects her nephew of wishing to make me an offer." She paused and considered it, then amended: "Or perhaps it is more correct to say that she wishes to deal with the possibility before Mr. Darcy can act in a way contrary to her designs."

At Charlotte's insistence, Elizabeth shared the details with her, and she did not stint on relating everything her ladyship said. Charlotte listened intently, and as was her wont, she gave little indication of her feelings. When Elizabeth finished her account, Charlotte sat back, a thoughtful frown fixed on her.

"That is extraordinary, Elizabeth."

"I know it is! To think that she thought proud, unbending Mr. Darcy might actually lower himself to offer for me! How is such a thing to be believed?"

"If you recall," replied Charlotte, "I have always thought Mr. Darcy looked at you often, and I have wondered at his apparent civility in visiting with such frequency."

"And yet, it is Mr. Darcy of whom we speak. I cannot suppose he regards me for any other reason than to catalog my faults more effectively."

"That is nothing less than silliness." Charlotte's firm tone surprised Elizabeth. "A man does not look on a woman he finds repulsive so often, Lizzy. Quite the opposite.

"I wonder, though," continued Charlotte, not allowing Elizabeth the opportunity to respond. "This business of Mr. Darcy's quick departure when he had given every sign he was settled here for the moment, and the evening we were to attend them at Rosings no less."

Mr. Collins still lamented the note canceling the invitation to the estate that evening, and that, in part, Elizabeth knew was what drove him to question if she had displeased Lady Catherine.

"Perhaps he refused to marry Miss de Bourgh," said Charlotte.

"It seems likely," replied Elizabeth. "But how *I* fit into this event is beyond my understanding."

"Lady Catherine coming here to speak to you is a sign *she*, at least, considers you a possible impediment to her plans. I know you do not think it possible, Elizabeth, but you should remember that Lady Catherine knows her nephew better than you or I do."

"I suppose she does," replied Elizabeth. "But I am inclined to believe she simply wished to assure herself that I was not a threat. I cannot imagine she saw anything in his behavior, else her own would have been much less restrained."

"In that, I suppose, I must confess you are correct." Charlotte paused and chuckled. "Had she any true notion of an attachment on

Mr. Darcy's side, she would have entered my home like an avenging angel, put the fear of God into my husband, and chased you back to Hertfordshire."

It was a fitting assessment of the lady's likely behavior and set Elizabeth to mirth. "I cannot but think you are entirely in the right, Charlotte."

"Thank you for that, Lizzy. Now, I wish to clarify one point—you said she demanded a promise that you would not accept Mr. Darcy's proposal should he offer one. Did you give her that promise?"

"Does it matter?" asked Elizabeth.

"Just humor me, my friend."

With a sigh, Elizabeth considered the question, remembering her conversation with Lady Catherine. At length, she shook her head.

"I did not explicitly state that I would not accept Mr. Darcy's proposal. I only informed her that I considered it impossible, and she accepted that as being as good as a promise."

"That is well then," said Charlotte.

"This is nonsensical, Charlotte. You suggest that Mr. Darcy might still offer for me when I know it is impossible. What does it matter if I promised?"

"It matters," replied Charlotte, "because that is a path that is still open to you, regardless of how impossible you believe it to be. I shall say nothing further of my opinion or the prospect of Mr. Darcy's future actions. I only ask you to keep an open mind."

Elizabeth laughed and promised she would. "As it is, I doubt I shall so much as see Mr. Darcy again, so it is of little matter. The promise is easy enough to give. The only reason I did not give Lady Catherine a similar assurance was because I found the very notion so ridiculous."

"Thank you, Elizabeth. Now, let us speak of something else, for I only have you for one more afternoon and evening, and would not waste a moment of it."

As eager to leave the subject as her friend, Elizabeth spent an agreeable afternoon in her friend's company. Maria appeared before dinner, informing them she had seen to her effects as Lady Catherine had instructed, provoking a grin between Charlotte and Elizabeth. Even Mr. Collins was not so objectionable that evening as he usually was, for he was silent more often than not, considering weighty matters.

As Elizabeth sought her bed that night, she reflected on her time in Kent, how it had proceeded in a manner she never would have expected. And tomorrow she was to depart. The separation from her friend was a matter of sorrow, but Elizabeth was eager to return to Jane and gain an accounting of how Mr. Bingley again entered her life.

CHAPTER III

"*J*ane is not here?"

Mrs. Gardiner smiled at Elizabeth's disbelief and ushered her to the stairs and from thence to her room. "She is not, Lizzy. When you have refreshed yourself, I shall tell you all." Then she looked back at Maria, who was following them in apparent interest: "Come, Maria, for I am certain you are as eager to wash as Elizabeth must be."

Maria smiled and nodded her agreement and allowed Mrs. Gardiner to lead her to another room next to Elizabeth's. The house her uncle owned was not the largest, but it could well accommodate a pair of young ladies for a single night. Elizabeth cared nothing for the house or any such considerations and hurried through her washing, eager to learn the reason for Jane's absence.

It was not to be supposed that Maria would remain in her room to rest. The news of Jane's absence could only come as a curiosity to the girl, particularly as she had heard of Mr. Bingley's appearance as Elizabeth had. Thus, Elizabeth was not surprised when they met in the hallway to return to the Gardiners' sitting-room, her pleasant face alight with curiosity.

"The matter is simple enough to explain," said Mrs. Gardiner, understanding at once that Elizabeth was wild for answers. "Your mother learned of some gossip of Mr. Bingley's imminent arrival at Netherfield Park, and she sent a letter, demanding Jane's immediate return."

Elizabeth frowned. "That is curious, Aunt. Did Mama not know of Mr. Bingley's visit here?"

The laughter in Mrs. Gardiner's face was infectious, and she said: "Would it have mattered? Even if she had, I have no doubt Maggie would have required your sister to return to her supervision, for no one but a mother could oversee such an important matter as the courtship of her eldest daughter."

It was so like her mother, that Elizabeth could not help but join her aunt's mirth. What a close likeness, indeed!

"Then I am to suppose that Mr. Bingley returned to Hertfordshire too?"

"The same morning that Jane returned," replied Mrs. Gardiner, her expression alight with mischief. "In the same carriage, for Mr. Bingley would hear nothing of Mr. Bennet sending his carriage when he meant to return to Netherfield Park himself."

Elizabeth had not thought her aunt's account could astonish her more, yet there it was. "And what of his family?"

"Of his eldest sister, I know nothing," said Mrs. Gardiner, "for I have never made her acquaintance. Miss Bingley accompanied her brother the first time he visited my home and was also present when they returned to Hertfordshire."

"Oh, that could not have been comfortable!" exclaimed Maria. "Miss Bingley is so hard, so severe, that I cannot imagine it would please her to return to Meryton."

It was a bit of understanding Elizabeth would not have expected of Maria. Then again, it made sense, for Elizabeth did not suppose anyone in Meryton could remain unaware of Miss Bingley's disinclination for their company, much less her overt disdain.

"There was one other accompanying Mr. Bingley that surprised me exceedingly."

"Even more than Mr. Bingley's sudden appearance?" asked Elizabeth, her mind focused on what her aunt had told her and failing to consider *of whom* her aunt might be speaking.

"From everything you told us, the gentleman was the last I might have expected to see in my sitting-room."

Elizabeth looked up sharply, finally understanding her aunt's suggestion, and Mrs. Gardiner nodded. "Yes, Lizzy, it was Mr. Darcy."

"Mr. Darcy!" said a shocked Maria. "Why, he must have come soon after he departed from Kent, for he left a week ago Thursday."

"He must not have wasted any time," said Mrs. Gardiner, "for by Monday he was sitting where you are now, with Mr. and Miss Bingley."

They discussed the matter for some more minutes, and yet Mrs. Gardiner was not explicit, for she gave no more information. The way she regarded Elizabeth, however, she was certain her aunt wished to say something more but was prevented by their present company. Maria listened and spoke without thought, speculating on the reason for Mr. Bingley's sudden appearance, and why Mr. Darcy had joined him. But when Mrs. Gardiner said nothing more, she became bored with the subject. Soon, she was happily ensconced with Mrs. Gardiner's daughters, playing with them, allowing Elizabeth and her aunt to converse more seriously.

"I must own, Lizzy, that I am quite disappointed." Mrs. Gardiner's wry smile took any sting from the words. "Given your testimony, I expected Mr. Darcy to be unapproachably proud. Yet, while Mr. Bingley focused his energies on Jane and Miss Bingley on doing what she could to separate them, they left me with the gentleman's company, and he was not uncivil."

"Incivility is not what I might have expected of him." Elizabeth paused and grimaced. "Then again, given his behavior in Meryton, it is not beyond his ability."

"And yet, I saw nothing of it. While the gentleman was not precisely comfortable, he was perfectly well behaved, and after we discovered we had something of which we could speak, he acquitted himself well."

Elizabeth could not imagine her surprise increasing, but the thought of proud Mr. Darcy speaking to the wife of a tradesman with perfect civility did the trick. "Something of which you could speak?"

"You are aware that I spent some years in Derbyshire when I was a girl?" At Elizabeth's nod, her aunt continued: "What you do not know is that the town I lived in, called Lambton, is no more than five miles from Pemberley, Mr. Darcy's estate."

"That *is* curious," replied Elizabeth. "Then did you know Mr. Darcy?"

"I did not, though I knew his mother by sight. But we know some of the same people in Lambton and its environs, and Mr. Darcy gave me newer intelligence of their doings than I had possessed. If you recall, your uncle and I are to tour the north this summer. I hope we will stop in Derbyshire for a time on our way to the lakes, for it is a wonderful country. And do you know what Mr. Darcy said when he heard this?"

It was with no little trepidation that Elizabeth waited for her aunt to tell her.

"He invited us, in a manner so earnest as to remove all possibility of misunderstanding, to stay at Pemberley while we are in the neighborhood."

Of all the astonishments of that day, this revelation was the greatest, for Elizabeth could not imagine what had made Mr. Darcy invite a woman he had only known for a matter of minutes. The wife of a tradesman, no less! How was such a thing to be understood?

"Lizzy." Her aunt's voice intruded on her confusion, and Elizabeth returned her attention to their discourse, noting her aunt's look of keen interest. "There is something else I have not told you yet, for Mr. Darcy asked after *you* in particular."

"I cannot imagine why he would have done so," replied Elizabeth. "For I saw him the day before he left Rosings Park."

Mrs. Gardiner leveled a long look at her. "No, Lizzy, he did not ask after your health or happiness. Rather, he conveyed your wellbeing to me, and then after we had exhausted the news of Lambton, he spent the rest of our time together asking me about you."

"About me?" Elizabeth's question came out as little more than a squeak.

"About you," echoed Mrs. Gardiner. "I had the distinct impression his questions were not idle. Thus, I have one question to ask you: is there something you have not told me of your acquaintance with Mr. Darcy?"

The question was so ridiculous that Elizabeth could not help but laugh, though more than a little of her current bewilderment manifest itself, making it more strained than she might have liked. Mr. Darcy, interested in Miss Elizabeth Bennet? The very notion was so preposterous that Elizabeth could not even understand how she should respond. Then a thought occurred to her, and she paled.

"Given your reaction, I assume there is nothing, yet it appears you have a notion."

"There is nothing, Aunt," said Elizabeth quickly. "I cannot imagine why Mr. Darcy might have deigned to ask about me to the extent you suggest when considering our history together."

"But?" prompted Aunt Gardiner.

"I hardly know," replied Elizabeth. "Yesterday, I received a most unexpected visit from Lady Catherine de Bourgh, Mr. Darcy's aunt."

"Please go on," said she when Elizabeth fell silent, feeling reluctant to speak further on the matter.

Elizabeth sighed, knowing she had no choice but to relate the scene at the parsonage to her aunt. "Lady Catherine called to speak to me, to assure herself that Mr. Darcy had made no overtures to me."

With a chuckle, Elizabeth added: "Lady Catherine, you see, has long desired that Mr. Darcy marry her daughter."

"And she suspected Mr. Darcy of favoring you?"

"Nothing so terrible as that," said Elizabeth with a lightness she did not feel. "Lady Catherine only wished to assure herself that I was not attempting to draw Mr. Darcy's attention, and I must suspect my status as a young and unattached woman led to her application, for she cannot have seen anything in his actions that led her to believe I was about to frustrate her designs. I assured her of the impossibility, and she thanked me and departed."

Mrs. Gardiner regarded Elizabeth for a long moment, her manner suggesting she was considering all Elizabeth had said. It was a dreadful moment for Elizabeth's nerves, for she respected and esteemed her aunt, counting her counsel among the most precious of her acquaintances. Yet she did not wish to disappoint her aunt, though she knew of no way Mrs. Gardiner would be upset with her unless it was because of her previous sportive manner with respect to Mr. Darcy in Meryton.

"This is most unusual, Lizzy," said Mrs. Gardiner at length. "You continue to claim your distaste for Mr. Darcy and the utter impossibility of his interest in you, yet I have evidence to the contrary. What am I supposed to believe?"

"I know not, Aunt, for this is incomprehensible to me."

"Then let me share what I have observed." Mrs. Gardiner ticked the points off on her fingers as she spoke. "Mr. Darcy comes with Mr. Bingley, and I suspect he informed his friend of Jane's presence, for Miss Bingley would not have done so. He shows himself to advantage with me, speaking most agreeably, asks after you, and in subsequent visits, treats my husband with the same warmth.

"At the same time, Lady Catherine applies to you, hoping to protect her cherished desire for Mr. Darcy to marry her daughter. Then, to top it off, Mr. Darcy returns to Hertfordshire with his friend, and if I have any notion of his intention, I suspect he means to put himself in your company again."

"For what purpose?" demanded Elizabeth.

Mrs. Gardiner watched her for a few moments and said: "For the same reason that any man will put himself into the company of any pretty young woman."

The words struck Elizabeth, for they were reminiscent of what Lady Catherine had said to her.

"And what if I do not favor Mr. Darcy?"

"That is your business, Lizzy." Mrs. Gardiner's gaze softened. "If Mr. Darcy is interested in you, I must commend his taste. I cannot tell you what to do or how to feel, but I urge you to be open to the possibility of an alliance with him if the gentleman makes any overtures."

"What of Lady Catherine?"

Mrs. Gardiner smiled and patted her hand. "It seems clear that Lady Catherine wishes this union to come about but has not the means to compel her nephew. As such, I suggest you do not allow her to prevent you from what you want. If that is Mr. Darcy, do not hesitate for her sake."

Then Mrs. Gardiner rose and, touching Elizabeth's cheek with affection, departed, leaving Elizabeth to her chaotic thoughts.

Darcy did not feel good about himself at present, and it was not a feeling to which he was accustomed, nor did he enjoy the sensation. Every time he returned to Longbourn, the feeling persisted, the knowledge that his behavior had been ridiculous, absurd, prejudiced, and haughty.

It was fortunate that Bingley was such a good sort, for he had not held Darcy's mistake against him, and he had not remained angry for long. It had been a side of Bingley that Darcy did not think he had ever seen before, for the moment the initial storm had subsided, Bingley had set his mind to considering how he might approach Miss Bennet. That he had proceeded long before Darcy might have ceased thinking of his options, with his typical disregard for rational thought had not surprised Darcy in the slightest, but he had been grateful, nonetheless. Bingley's sisters, however . . . .

Darcy grimaced at himself in the mirror in his room. Miss Bingley was the reason Darcy was lingering in his room, having refreshed himself after returning from Longbourn. Since informing Bingley of Miss Bennet's presence in London, he had learned that Miss Bingley had a shrill voice and a piercing screech, such as he had never thought to hear from her. The woman's behavior in his company had always been above reproach, though Darcy had always known she fancied him for a husband. That was now proven to be an act, for he had seen an aspect of her that did not please him at all.

The reasons for Darcy's dissatisfaction with himself were varied, and they centered on his behavior in the neighborhood the previous year and his judgment of the Bennet family in particular. Some of his opinions were not incorrect, and he was certain even Miss Elizabeth would confess it. The younger girls were wild and in serious need of a firm hand, and Mrs. Bennet was a woman difficult to tolerate, loud and obvious in her machinations. Darcy had almost quit the place never to return when the woman had tried to push her youngest daughter at him.

Mr. Bennet, for a wonder, had intervened, much to Darcy and Miss Lydia's mutual satisfaction and relief. Of the Bennet patriarch, Darcy had begun to think better. While he could not countenance the man's habitual divorce from the needs of his family, a few occasions in his company had taught him that Mr. Bennet was intelligent, a man after his own heart in many ways. While his humor was a little biting for Darcy's taste, he thought he could esteem the man with tolerable ease.

And perhaps the greatest surprise was the middle girl, for Miss Mary, contrary to Darcy's opinion of her being close to a bluestocking, was instead only overlooked. She too was clearly intelligent, as several conversations with her had revealed. If her choice of literature was a little too dry and moralizing for Darcy's taste, he thought she wanted direction more than anything else. Darcy had enjoyed his time with her beyond what he might have thought and had even given her a few suggestions of reading material he thought would benefit her. That Miss Mary had accepted with her usual gravity and promised to look into them proved she was not beyond accepting advice.

With a sigh, Darcy took one last look at himself in the mirror and girded his courage for Miss Bingley's company. While he might wish to remain in his room, he knew it was not good manners to do so, and as much of his recent behavior had been revealed to be lacking in courtesy, he was determined to learn from his mistakes. Before he descended, however, he came across his friend.

"So, Darcy," said Bingley, his usual ebullience on full display, "how did you find the Bennet family today?"

"The same as we found them yesterday," said Darcy, more than a hint of wryness coming out in his tone. "I should not suppose that your opinion differs greatly from my own.

"And before you say it, I confess without reservation that I was entirely mistaken about Miss Bennet's regard for you." Darcy gave his friend a grin he could not quite feel and added: "That was the point of speaking with you in the first place, was it not?"

"It was, and I thank you for it, my friend."

Bingley stepped close and clasped Darcy's shoulder. "I promise I shall not hold this over your head forever. You must excuse me at present, for I am feeling all the justification at being correct." A shadow crossed Bingley's face. "I only wish I had stood by my convictions."

"Perhaps we have all learned a lesson," replied Darcy. "I know I am inept when attempting to divine a woman's feelings, and you have learned you should trust your own judgment."

"And what of my sister?"

Darcy could not help his grimace, and he could see at once that Bingley agreed with him in every particular.

"I shall not make you say it, my friend," said Bingley. "Caroline has learned nothing—that much is abundantly clear. I hope she will keep a civil tongue in her head, for it will not take much to provoke me to send her to my family in the north and wash my hands of her."

With a nod, Darcy regarded his friend curiously. "What of the Hursts? It surprised me to find they were not in London with you."

"Hurst received word of his father's illness. The old man bedevils him at every turn—I suspect he hopes this will finally be the time he will give up the ghost and make Hurst the master of his estate."

It was one of the few subjects of which Hurst willingly spoke, so Darcy had heard all about his feelings of exasperation for his father. It was a subject that did not bear repeating.

"I must return to my room," said Bingley. "But I shall join you in the sitting-room momentarily."

When Darcy hesitated, Bingley laughed and slapped his shoulder. "I believe Caroline is now in her bedchamber so you should emerge from a moment of solitude in this house unscathed."

Grateful to hear it, Darcy accepted and made his way below stairs. When he entered the sitting-room, he was thus surprised to see it already occupied. Darcy did not know where Bingley had obtained his intelligence regarding his sister's movements, but it appeared he did not know as much as he thought.

"Mr. Darcy!" cried the woman as soon as he entered the room. "How good of you to join me, for I am quite confused about what has happened these past days. Will you not explain why you saw fit to inform my brother of Miss Bennet's presence in town when we had gone to such trouble to separate them?"

This was the main reason for Darcy's disquiet. The knowledge that he had injured Miss Bennet and had misled his friend when Bingley had counted on him for good advice did not sit well with him. Further, the knowledge that Miss Bingley had lied, and misrepresented her brother to Miss Bennet filled him with revulsion; Darcy had by now heard of her attempts to end the acquaintance with Miss Bennet, knew of her lies when she had told her brother Miss Bennet had not written, disapproved of her calculated delay for a full three weeks before she had returned Miss Bennet's visit. If Darcy had behaved poorly, Miss Bingley's behavior was no less than reprehensible. Miss Bingley's selfishness was now bared to Darcy's gaze, and he liked the woman far less for it than he had. He had always known she was more than a little high in the instep, but he had never thought her capable of such harm as she had perpetrated against Miss Bennet.

"Tell me, Miss Bingley," said Darcy at length, ignoring her question, "have you truly looked at Miss Bennet? Have you not seen how we have injured her by our actions, how we hurt your brother by keeping him away from her?"

"*If* Miss Bennet was of any consequence," snarled she, "I might feel some regret for my actions. But I do not. Miss Bennet is in no way worthy to be my sister, and now it appears as if all my efforts to separate my brother from her and her abominable family have been for naught. Had you not betrayed me, I would, even now, be guiding my brother to some other woman more worthy of him, one who will help us in society and not bring him repentance and regret."

"I neither require nor wish for your guidance, Caroline," said Bingley as he entered the room.

While one might expect Miss Bingley's embarrassment at being overheard, she was too far gone in fury to pay such extraneous subjects any heed. Bingley, it seemed, had turned over a new leaf with his sister, for he did not allow her to respond.

"As for why Darcy informed me of Miss Bennet's presence, it is because he is a loyal friend. That is more than I can say for my own blood in this instance."

"Charles—"

"If you mean to assert yet again that she is not worthy of me, I suggest you hold your tongue."

Miss Bingley's mouth snapped closed, but her glare never dimmed.

"It appears, Caroline dear," said Bingley, more than a hint of scorn in his voice, "that I have ignored your airs for too long. How you can conclude that an education at a seminary and a dowry make you the Bennets' superior in society, I cannot comprehend, for *they* are gentlefolk."

"What of their behavior?"

"The behavior of some is suspect, but even you must own that charge cannot be laid at Miss Bennet's door. Regardless, I find I do not care for your arrogance, and your attempt to continue to defend the indefensible offends me. If you cannot remain silent, I suggest you absent yourself. When you have regained your composure, you may return."

Miss Bingley gave him a hateful glare, but she did not remain in their company after such a set down. It was amusing to note that she did not even excuse herself before she stalked from the room in high dudgeon. Darcy found he did not repine her absence or lament her incivility, for he had been near to calling her to order had Bingley not been of a mind to do it himself.

"I apologize, Darcy," said Bingley, turning to him. "I must have misunderstood the housekeeper, for I thought she intended to remain in her room."

"Perhaps the desire to induce me to account for myself drew her out," said Darcy, waving away his friend's apology. "It is no trouble, Bingley."

"I *am* grateful for your integrity, Darcy," said Bingley. "I know I have said it more than once, but it is true all the same."

"It is something I should have done sooner. If you wish to show your appreciation, I wonder if you will grant me a boon."

"Anything," averred his friend.

Darcy chuckled and admonished: "It is always better to learn what boon another will ask before agreeing, my friend."

"I am feeling far too happy, Darcy. Name it, and it shall be done."

"I should like to invite my sister to Netherfield."

That seemed to catch Bingley by surprise. "It was my understanding you preferred to keep your sister at a distance from mine."

"That is Georgiana's desire," replied Darcy, "though I have long understood your sister's treatment of mine stems from her desire to impress me."

"And a foolish notion it is," said Bingley with a snort. "If you think she can endure Caroline's ill humor, I have no objection." Bingley laughed as another thought came to him. "Caroline will usually anticipate Miss Darcy's coming with scarcely hidden eagerness. On this occasion, however, I suspect it will anger her more than anything."

Bingley paused and gave him a shrewd look. "If you will excuse my saying so, I suspect there is some other reason you wish to invite her, Darcy, and it is not because of Caroline. There has been something odd in your behavior to the Bennets, and I would know what it is if you are willing to share."

As it happened, Darcy did not care to inform his friend of his intentions. But Bingley would learn of them before long, for Darcy was determined to make his move as soon as Miss Elizabeth's acceptance of his suit was a reasonable surety. Perhaps before if he thought he could persuade her. Thus, it seemed there was little reason to keep the matter from Bingley.

Thus, they sat and discussed it for the rest of the afternoon. To say it astonished Bingley was an understatement, but soon he saw the humor of the situation, and he was not hesitant to express it. The best part of the afternoon was that Miss Bingley did not make an appearance again until dinner, and even then, she ignored them except for a few aggrieved looks. Darcy found he could endure her silence cheerfully.

CHAPTER IV

"*N*ot all at once! I cannot understand when you all speak at once!"

"Elizabeth is correct," said Mr. Bennet, interrupting his wife and daughters with his usual amusement. "Perhaps it would be best if you allowed Elizabeth to gain her feet before you all inundate her with your news."

It could not be supposed that the ladies who comprised Elizabeth's family would fall silent without protest. But her father's admonishment had the desired effect, as they quieted, slowly, and allowed Elizabeth to enter the house, though they were hard on her heels. Mrs. Bennet, Lydia, and Kitty, Elizabeth could understand, but even Mary appeared eager to share her news. Once she had gained the vestibule, Elizabeth turned and regarded them all warmly.

"If you will allow me a moment, I shall return to my room and wash, and then join you in the sitting-room."

"Hurry, Lizzy," said her mother, and for once Mrs. Bennet's usual excitability did not overcome her. "I shall send for refreshments."

Bemused by her mother's restraint, Elizabeth made her way to her room, hurrying through her ablutions, before returning down the stairs to her family. Inside she was bursting with curiosity, for she had never seen her family so eager to share the news of the neighborhood. Mr. Bingley's return was among the things that she expected to hear, and she could not help but wonder if Mr. Darcy provoked some of the rest. Elizabeth could not have imagined how correct she was.

"Lizzy!" exclaimed Mrs. Bennet, her excitement having returned while Elizabeth was absent. "Come here so we can tell you all the news!"

"Of course, Mama," replied Elizabeth, sitting in the indicated place near her mother. "This must be news of the gravest import, for I have never seen you all in this state."

"Mr. Bingley has returned!" said Mrs. Bennet, her voice filled with rapture.

"So I have heard," observed Elizabeth. "You forget I was in London yesterday and heard of the man's recent movements. I also know he visited Jane in London."

"Yes, well," faltered Mrs. Bennet. "It is better that Jane returned home to receive Mr. Bingley for there is no better place for a courtship than in the bosom of her family."

Elizabeth turned an expressive glance on Jane, who blushed but nodded. "Mr. Bingley has been very attentive since he returned."

While Jane said nothing more, Elizabeth was certain there was much more to tell. But she could not say so in company with the rest of her family, and Mrs. Bennet was not about to cede the floor, regardless. For some minutes, she spoke of Mr. Bingley, his appearance, his continued handsome countenance, her expectations of a match with her eldest daughter, and other such comments, much of which Elizabeth had already heard. Elizabeth attempted to listen patiently, wondering if this was all her mother had to say, even as she noted her sisters appeared eager to add to her account. Then Mrs. Bennet shifted topics and said something that truly shocked her.

"And did you know that Mr. Darcy returned with Mr. Bingley?" asked she.

"I did," replied Elizabeth, and that was all her mother allowed her to say.

"He has been the most obliging, the most charming man since his return." A shadow passed over Mrs. Bennet's face and she shot a look at Jane. "Other than Mr. Bingley, of course. But Mr. Darcy's affability was a great surprise."

"Mr. Darcy?" asked Elizabeth. "He has been friendly?"

"He has." Mrs. Bennet peered at her, a hint of a frown oversetting her features. "As I recall, you saw Mr. Darcy in Kent, did you not?"

"I did," affirmed Elizabeth.

"Then I wonder why you did not inform me of the changes in him in your letters." Mrs. Bennet shook her head. "Regardless, I declare I have never met such a consummate gentleman as Mr. Darcy, and this after he gave such a poor impression this previous autumn!"

"Mr. Darcy *has* acquitted himself well," said Mr. Bennet. "He can be standoffish when you first speak to him, but he improves upon acquaintance. Tomorrow, Darcy and Bingley are to come to Longbourn and shoot with me."

"That *is* a surprise," replied Elizabeth, not needing to feign the shock in her voice.

"You mean he was not the same in Kent?" demanded Mrs. Bennet.

"I noted no significant alteration," replied Elizabeth, "though he was more attentive to the parsonage than I might have expected."

"I care nothing for Mr. Darcy!" cried Lydia, finally unable to hold her tongue. "Do you not know what he has done to poor Wickham?"

Elizabeth turned a sharp look on her sister. She had not so much as thought of Mr. Wickham in more than a week, yet the old offense for another she had felt when Mr. Wickham had told her of his history with Mr. Darcy returned, though a pale shadow of what it once had been. If Mr. Darcy had told Mr. Bingley of Jane's presence in London as she suspected, he had redeemed himself in that respect. But what of his behavior toward Mr. Wickham?

"What do you mean?"

"Why, Mr. Wickham is gone at Mr. Darcy's instigation!" wailed Lydia. "And we do not know what they have done to him!"

"Perhaps, Daughter," said Mr. Bennet, "you should allow me to relate this tale, for visions of dashing officers still dance in your head, and you are in no condition to do it justice."

Lydia glared at her father, but she did not protest. Thus, Elizabeth turned to Mr. Bennet, her questioning look prompting a chuckle.

"Your sister is generally correct, but she omits much of the context."

The huff from her younger sister informed them of her opinion, but Mr. Bennet did not spare a glance for her.

"Late last week, a colonel of the regulars came to Meryton and took Mr. Wickham into custody."

"I was there when it happened!" exclaimed Lydia. "He just sauntered up to Mr. Wickham and clapped him in chains without so much as a by your leave! And Mr. Wickham did nothing to provoke it!"

"Peace, Lydia," growled Mr. Bennet. "If you continue to interrupt,

I shall never finish my account."

It was evident to them all that Lydia was impatient to enlist Elizabeth to her side of the dispute. Elizabeth did not know what to think. Colonel Fitzwilliam must have been the army colonel to apprehend Mr. Wickham, but for what purpose Elizabeth could not say. Surely the genial man she had met in Kent would not allow his official position to be used for such nefarious purposes as the persecution of a man his cousin did not like.

"Thank you," said Mr. Bennet, still eyeing his daughter, his gaze suggesting she had best not interrupt again. He turned back to Elizabeth. "It appears Mr. Wickham was doing nothing wrong *at the time* of his arrest. However, this army colonel and his men escorted Wickham to the regiment's headquarters and there he spoke with Colonel Forster. While no one knows of what they discussed in that meeting, the colonel investigated and discovered that Mr. Wickham owed money to every reputable tradesman in Meryton."

"He owes money in town?" asked Elizabeth with a gasp.

Her father gave her a grim nod. "Yes, he does. And the amounts are such that it could not be a simple error as he tried to plead. Then Mr. Darcy involved himself in the situation."

"Mr. Darcy?" gasped Elizabeth.

"He did," said Mrs. Bennet. "According to my sister Phillips, Mr. Darcy denounced Mr. Wickham to the colonel and showed receipts he holds in Mr. Wickham's name as proof of his assertions. Mr. Darcy then paid all Mr. Wickham's debts in Meryton and had him taken away."

Mrs. Bennet sniffed her disdain. "Good riddance to him, I say, for he has been a snake in the grass, waiting to strike at us all."

"But Mama!" exclaimed Lydia. "Mr. Wickham is so handsome and good. I am certain this was all some elaborate scheme on Mr. Darcy's part to discredit him. We all know how much Mr. Darcy hates him."

"You may think that, Lydia," said Mr. Bennet, eyeing Lydia with more asperity than usual. "If it brings you comfort, you may believe it to your dying day. Can I assume you are telling the truth when you informed me that Mr. Wickham has not trifled with you?"

Lydia colored and nodded, falling silent. Elizabeth was bewildered.

"Are there reports of Mr. Wickham dishonoring ladies of the neighborhood?"

"It appears matters did not go that far," said Mr. Bennet, with a shake of his head. "Yet, in the aftermath, several girls of the town came forward and reported the man's efforts to seduce them. It is a wonder nothing more severe than flirting has occurred. Lydia was thick with Mr. Wickham, but she will not confess to anything inappropriate with him."

"That is because there is nothing to confess," insisted Lydia. "Do you take me for some sort of scarlet woman? I would never allow a man such liberties!"

"I am happy to hear it, Lydia," replied Mr. Bennet. "But your behavior sometimes leads one to believe that you would sell your soul for a bit of a lark. This is serious business."

Lydia nodded but would not speak again.

"I can scarcely believe such reports of Mr. Wickham!" exclaimed Elizabeth. "There was such an expression of goodness in his countenance."

"Aye, that is the most dangerous sort of man," agreed her father. "A man who wears a sign proclaiming his depravity cannot be feared, but the snake who speaks with a sibilant tongue and pretty manners may cause much damage before the truth is discovered."

Elizabeth gasped as a thought occurred to her. "With behavior such as this, we must suspect now falsehood in Mr. Wickham's account of his betrayal at Mr. Darcy's hand."

Mr. Bennet regarded her and gave her a slow, pleased nod. "It is good you have apprehended that fact, Lizzy. To the best of my knowledge, Mr. Darcy has not spoken on the subject, and I would not dream of asking him. But I believe recent events have led our neighbors to alter their opinions of him."

Difficult though it was to fathom, Elizabeth nodded, agreeing with his assessment. As for the rest of her family, Mrs. Bennet sat upright, her satisfaction plain to see, Mary was disapproving, Lydia hunched over and unmoved, and Kitty seemed to waver between siding with Lydia and agreeing with her father. Jane, of course, was serene, but there was a measure of approval in her as if she had confronted the possibility of evil in a young man known to them all and been saddened by what they found but satisfied the danger had been neutralized.

"I still cannot believe it," muttered Lydia into the silence.

"You may believe what you wish," said Mr. Bennet. "But Mr. Darcy has saved this community a lot of trouble, and I, for one, am indebted to him."

"Mr. Darcy has shown himself to far greater advantage than any of us would have thought," said Mary, speaking for the first time. "He was kind and attentive to me when we spoke, and even recommended a few books he thought I might enjoy."

As if to demonstrate what she said, Mary held the book she was holding, and Elizabeth noted it was a volume of poetry from her father's library. Elizabeth looked at her askance, and Mary was happy to respond.

"Mr. Darcy is very learned and was willing to discuss various subjects with me. On the whole, I have found his suggestions worthy, though some have not been completely to my taste. He encouraged me to widen my reading material, and to enlarge my mind."

"The man has accomplished in a week what I could not do in nearly twenty years," said Mr. Bennet, regarding his middle daughter with a fondness Elizabeth did not think she had ever seen from him. "You may retrieve anything you like from my library, Mary, so long as you return it in the same state you borrowed it."

"Of course, Papa," replied Mary, clutching her book to her breast.

The conversation continued from there, and Elizabeth heard many more accounts of the doings of Mr. Darcy and Mr. Bingley. While she might have attributed most of what they said to Mr. Bingley, that Mr. Darcy had been so open was a matter she could not quite comprehend. What could have induced the man to change so drastically in so short a time?

Later, when night fell and Elizabeth sought her room, Elizabeth took thought again for her elder sister, and as they had often done since they were girls, she joined Jane in her room for a long evening conference. As they snuggled together in Jane's bed, Elizabeth listened to her sister speak of Mr. Bingley, her hopes newly awakened from hibernation, her certainty the man meant to pay her the highest compliment now he had returned. Elizabeth was ecstatic for her sister, but the nagging question of how Mr. Bingley had learned of her presence in London gnawed at her until she could not wait for Jane to speak of it.

"It was Mr. Darcy, Lizzy," said Jane when Elizabeth asked. "When he returned from Kent, he went to Mr. Bingley at once and informed him of my presence in London, apologizing for his error. According to Mr. Bingley, Mr. Darcy thought I was indifferent to him—this led him to advise Mr. Bingley against returning last December."

"Oh, I am certain it was nothing more than an error," said Elizabeth with some heat.

"If you recall, Lizzy," said Jane, meeting her asperity with mildness, "Charlotte told you that I should show my esteem more openly, and I cannot but conclude she was correct. I am greatly in Mr. Darcy's debt, for I doubt I could anticipate this happy ending without his intervention."

That took the wind out of Elizabeth's sails neatly, and she sighed and smiled at her sister. "I suppose you must be correct, Jane. But I must wonder about what has come over Mr. Darcy. When I said I had noticed no change in him while we were both in Kent, I was not dissembling."

"Perhaps something you said informed him of the truth," suggested Jane.

The memory of her walk with Colonel Fitzwilliam, how he had told her of Mr. Darcy's efforts to separate Jane from Mr. Bingley, crossed Elizabeth's mind. Could Colonel Fitzwilliam have seen something of her turmoil and reported it to Mr. Darcy? It was possible, she supposed, though she had thought at the time the colonel had not suspected anything amiss when she had spoken of a headache. The gentlemen had left that very day, as she recalled. Would such a nebulous event have caused Mr. Darcy to set off for London at once to rectify his error? It seemed unlikely, but what other explanation did she have?

Then there was Lady Catherine's curious confrontation with Elizabeth and suspicion of Mr. Darcy's potential interest in her. Was it all connected? Elizabeth thought it must be, but at present, she could not see the links in the chain.

"What is it, Lizzy?" asked Jane. "Do you know something?"

Elizabeth shook her head. "Nothing more than a suspicion, and a tenuous one at that. I am more interested in this situation with Mr. Bingley and, in particular, with his sisters. Have they also returned to Meryton?"

"Only Miss Bingley."

Jane's closed answer told her nothing, for while Miss Bingley was the instigator between them, she had not thought Mrs. Hurst any warmer to their brother's interest in Elizabeth's dear sister. When Elizabeth did not remove her gaze, Jane sighed and lead back against the headboard.

"Miss Bingley has said little since her return, Lizzy. But her air has been altogether insolent, disobliging, vexed, and shrewish. The way she behaved in London, I find I cannot esteem or trust her as much as I once did. That is unfortunate, but I cannot repine my caution, for I do not wish to be taken in again."

"I am pleased that you see it so," said Elizabeth. "While I would not advise you to shun Miss Bingley, she must prove herself to you. There is no obligation for you to accept any overtures she might make until she does."

"I cannot agree more," replied Jane. "Now, will you not tell me what you thought when you fell silent a moment ago?"

They spent several hours together before falling asleep. Jane agreed with Elizabeth's contention that she did not have all the information, but she also concurred with Elizabeth's opinion that the two matters were connected. It seemed the link could be nothing other than Mr. Darcy, and until the gentleman saw fit to explain, there was little they could do to understand. As Elizabeth dropped into slumber, she determined she would look for an opportunity to ask him; it was not something to blurt out when in company so she would need to take care.

When Darcy went to Longbourn the day after Miss Elizabeth's return from London, anxiety ruled his mind. Torturing himself with thoughts of what Miss Elizabeth thought of him, he rode next to Bingley, wondering if he would ever survive that day. His friend's encouragement was welcome, but Darcy did not hear most of what Bingley had to say on the subject, so focused was he on what lay ahead.

His future life free of Lady Catherine's overbearing influence and Anne as a wife did *not* depend on Miss Elizabeth's acceptance of his suit. This Darcy knew, for he could defy Lady Catherine's edicts and resist her insistence, even if it would be more difficult if he remained unmarried. But Darcy was quickly concluding that his future happiness *was* dependent on Miss Elizabeth when he finally decided the time was right for his proposal.

"Ah, Bingley, Darcy," said Mr. Bennet when they entered his study, Darcy following his friend, reluctance in every step. "If you will indulge me, there is a matter I must attend to before we may depart. In the meantime, will you not visit with the ladies?"

The grin with which he made his suggestion met a matching one from Bingley, as Bennet had expected. The way his eyes lingered on Darcy, however, suggested the man knew more than he was saying. Or was Darcy seeing phantasms where there were none? He did not know whether to be eager or anxious at the thought of braving Miss Elizabeth's company again, but he dutifully followed Bingley to the sitting-room.

The ladies were all within when they arrived, and Darcy's eyes immediately sought out Miss Elizabeth, who rose with her mother and sisters when they entered. Miss Elizabeth's returning regard appeared puzzled, but she said nothing as Bingley greeted the ladies and sat near Miss Bennet. Had Darcy realized he was giving the same impression he gave last autumn—and this after he had taken pains to alter his behavior since returning—he might have endeavored to speak more. As it was, his confusion concerning Miss Elizabeth prevented him from even thinking to open his mouth. But it did not prevent him from choosing a seat near her with an absence of thought.

When he sat, Miss Elizabeth made some comment, and Darcy replied with something incomprehensible, and for a moment, he could think of nothing to say. Then, out of desperation, he noted how Bingley was close to Miss Bennet and was speaking with her animatedly, and said:

"Bingley and Miss Bennet appear to be getting on well, would you not say?"

Miss Elizabeth regarded him critically, such that he felt like a boy when his father had reprimanded him for some mischief. "I beg your pardon, Mr. Darcy, for I do not mean to offend. But I understand you did not always agree with that sentiment."

"I am not offended," replied Darcy evenly. "It is nothing less than the truth."

"Then why did you inform Mr. Bingley of her presence in London?"

"Because I realized I was wrong." Darcy turned and regarded her, drinking in the sight of her dark hair, her expressive eyes, and the creamy smoothness of her skin. "No man is perfect if you recall; I am no more immune to misstep than any other."

The corners of Miss Elizabeth's eyes crinkled in amusement. "But has it not been the study of your life to avoid those weaknesses which often expose a strong understanding to ridicule?"

Remembering the exchange, Darcy grinned and replied: "Such as vanity and pride, yes. Perhaps I am afflicted by the second more than the first, but I should like to overcome both as best I can."

"It appears your behavior these previous days has spoken to your improvement."

"I am happy to receive your family's endorsement," replied Darcy. "As for your sister, I would like you to understand I never intended to hurt her with my actions. My motivation has always been Bingley's happiness."

She regarded him for a long moment, her scrutiny discomfiting him. "Do you suppose that is within your purview as a friend?"

"Bingley is several years younger than I am, Miss Elizabeth. He is an excellent friend, and we have grown so close that I have sometimes considered him with affection akin to a younger brother. Does an elder brother not wish the best for the younger?"

A slow nod comprised her response. "When you put it that way, I understand."

"Thank you, Miss Elizabeth. Given your sister's involvement, your resentment is no mystery."

"Jane has forgiven whatever unintentional damage you wrought. Can I do anything less?"

"When you put it that way, perhaps I should thank Miss Bennet for softening your opinion of me."

Miss Elizabeth cocked her head to the side, but she did not speak for a long moment. What she could be thinking Darcy could not say, but he became aware that most of the other ladies were watching them, intent upon their interaction. A moment later, Darcy realized he had perhaps given the impression of interest in his choice of a place to sit, not to mention his interest in rehabilitating his reputation when he had returned. That he intended everything they suspected and more did not bear consideration. He had not intended to give such an impression, not until after he was certain of her reception.

"In the matter of Jane," said Miss Elizabeth, returning his attention to her, "it appears you have acquitted yourself well, and I cannot argue with the result. Jane is as happy as I have ever seen her.

"But there is another matter that confuses me."

"Oh?" asked Darcy, an awful surety of what she meant entering his mind.

"Mr. Wickham," said she, confirming his suspicions. "I understand his actions in Meryton damned him, to say nothing of your testimony of his behavior before he came. I can only thank you for exposing him and righting his wrongs."

"It was my responsibility," replied Darcy simply. "I have so often contented myself with ignoring him that I forgot what havoc an unfettered Wickham can unleash on those he misuses."

"That is an interesting contention, Mr. Darcy, and one I think I might contradict on another occasion. In this instance, however, I am curious about something else. Much of Mr. Wickham's words have been proven lies and I should not wonder if this will not as well. But the one matter for which I have yet to hear an explanation is his charge that you denied him a living left to him by your father. Would it be an imposition to ask after the truth of that aspect of his tale?"

"Well, gentlemen," said Mr. Bennet, neatly interrupting them as he entered the room. "Shall we depart?"

Bingley agreed readily and rose to join him. Darcy was slower, Miss Elizabeth's question still ringing in his mind, while equally distracted by Mr. Bennet's knowing look at his position by the man's second daughter. Darcy ignored the second for the moment to concentrate on the first consideration.

"It appears I must go, Miss Elizabeth. Before I do so, however, I will refute what Wickham said, and have proof of my assertions."

"Your word is proof enough, Mr. Darcy."

Darcy was flattered, and he grinned to show it. "Thank you. Then I look forward to explaining the last of Wickham's behavior to you when the opportunity presents itself.

As they left the house for their sport, Darcy reflected that the first meeting had gone better than he might have expected. The warm feeling of hope welled up within his breast.

CHAPTER V

"Why does *she* come here? It is not as if any of us misunderstand her disapproval of us."

"Lower your voice, Lydia," said Elizabeth, though privately she agreed with her sister. "Whatever we think of Miss Bingley, she is our guest at present. It would not do to speak in such a way as to offend her."

Lydia huffed, but she said nothing further, instead choosing to sit with Kitty, where they put their heads together in whispered conversation. The way their eyes were often upon Miss Bingley resulted in any inability to hide the subject of their discourse, but as Miss Bingley only glanced at them, her glare an indication of contempt, Elizabeth supposed there was no need to call them to order.

But the question foremost in Elizabeth's mind was the same her sister had posed—why had Miss Bingley come? The gentlemen were greeting Mr. Bennet in his library and were not present, leaving Miss Bingley to greet the ladies alone. Jane, whose new understanding of Miss Bingley did not move her to unkindness, had greeted the woman and attempted to make her feel at ease. Not that her efforts would meet any success, for, in Elizabeth's opinion, Miss Bingley was determined to be displeased. Even now, when she sat with Jane, the civility she had often showed when in Hertfordshire before was absent, leaving behind a sort of arrogant forbearance. Had Jane been unaware of Miss Bingley's opinion, Elizabeth could not imagine she would now be in any doubt.

In the three days since Elizabeth's return, she had been in company with the Netherfield party often, for there had been some congress between the two estates daily. Yet those at Netherfield always came to Longbourn, for it was a tacit acknowledgment between them all that Miss Bingley would not greet them with anything resembling welcome should they presume to brave her displeasure in her domain. But she had also not come to Longbourn until that day, which begged the question of why she had come now.

These days had been a test for Elizabeth's understanding, for, after that first day when Mr. Darcy had been closed, he had displayed his newfound civility for all to see. They had had no further opportunity to speak of Mr. Wickham, and Elizabeth had concluded it was unnecessary. The man's own actions had condemned him, such that anything he said was now suspect. Yet Elizabeth was certain Mr. Darcy would broach the subject again, for she had gained a healthy respect for his determination to do what he said he would.

And the changes in her family toward the gentleman were striking! Mrs. Bennet was now apt to praise him to the skies, and even Lydia, whose offense for Mr. Wickham had persisted, had now grudgingly concluded that he was an estimable sort of gentleman. Was there some purpose behind Mr. Darcy's shocking alteration? If there was, Elizabeth could not imagine what it could be.

Elizabeth did not know how it happened, but a few moments later, she found herself nearby Miss Bingley, as Jane had left the room, though for what reason she could not say. It appeared Miss Bingley would not say anything to her, for her one glance at Elizabeth spoke volumes of her disdain. Unwilling to allow the woman to affect her behavior, Elizabeth endeavored to make some comment, however brief.

"I hope your stay at Netherfield is comfortable."

As comments went, it was far more banal than Elizabeth usually allowed herself. Miss Bingley sniffed and replied: "Netherfield is . . . adequate."

When it appeared she would say nothing further, Elizabeth tried again: "I hope your sister is well. I understand the Hursts are in the north."

"They are." Miss Bingley said nothing further, apparently wishing to remain silent. A moment later, however, her mouth opened again, though unwillingly. "They have gone to Hurst's family estate in Norfolk."

"Have you been there? I have rarely been to the sea, but I have always enjoyed it when I have gone."

"The estate is not three miles from the shore," replied Miss Bingley. "It is not a place I wish to visit often, but it is . . . adequate, I suppose."

Elizabeth hid a smile from her companion, not that Miss Bingley would have noticed, as she refused to look at her. The turn of her phrase in discussing both Norfolk and Netherfield suggested she would consider nothing less than The Queen's House itself acceptable! Or perhaps a lesser property might be sufficient for her pretensions of grandeur, but only if it was in Derbyshire, and only if inhabited by a particular gentleman of means and standing.

A thought seemed to come to the woman, and she turned to Elizabeth. "Do you know that Georgiana Darcy is to come to stay with us?"

"Is she?" asked Elizabeth. "Mr. Darcy must anticipate her coming."

"Of course, he does," said Miss Bingley. It did not escape her notice that Miss Bingley's tone which had previously been bordering on rude now exuded smug satisfaction. "Mr. Darcy *is*, after all, very close to his sister.

"And I am scarcely less fond of her, for she is truly an excellent creature. All the Darcy and Fitzwilliam poise, excellence of temper and behavior, and nobility are present in her. I could not be fonder of her had she been *my* sister."

"She truly sounds like a wondrous young woman, Miss Bingley," said Elizabeth. "I can scarcely wait to be introduced to her."

The woman's demeanor altered in an instant, her previous boasting turning sour, her speech becoming silent. She glared as if she suspected Elizabeth of conspiring to corrupt young Georgiana Darcy the moment she arrived. Then she sniffed and turned away.

"It would be best if you did not hope for such a thing, Eliza."

"Why might that be?" asked Elizabeth, feeling hilarity well up within her. "Mr. Darcy and your brother have come to Longbourn every day since my return to Hertfordshire, and nearly every day before, based on my family's testimony. Can I not assume that he will not also bring his sister?"

"As you do not know the gentleman as well as I do, it is unsurprising you would think that."

Miss Bingley's conceit was nigh unendurable, for all the

amusement she provoked.

"Mr. Darcy, you see," continued she, leaning closer as if to impart a secret, "takes great care for his sister, and will not expose her to just *anybody*. She is of the highest quality, such that he must take care, so she is not unduly *influenced* by disruptive elements, not in keeping with how he is raising her."

The look Miss Bingley directed at Kitty and Lydia, and her glance at Elizabeth herself, informed her of the meaning of her crass statement. Had her inference been in any way opaque, that was.

"Then I suspect he will continue to take care," replied Elizabeth. "Of course, if he considers certain individuals as appropriate acquaintances for himself, I cannot imagine he would prevent his sister from mingling with them. I suppose we must wait and see." Miss Bingley's look was unfriendly, to say the least, but the sound of the gentlemen approaching the sitting-room distracted her away from whatever retort she was about to make. When the door opened, Mr. Bingley stepped into the room, followed by Mr. Darcy. Mr. Bingley glanced about in seeming disappointment for Jane's continued absence, but Mr. Darcy looked at Elizabeth herself. Whether it was the gentleman's actions that provoked her Elizabeth could not say, but Miss Bingley rose at once and approached them, speaking to them in low tones, her gestures betraying the forcefulness of whatever she was saying.

No doubt she wished to browbeat them into returning to Netherfield Park at once. That or her purpose was to persuade Mr. Darcy not to make her appear a fool by keeping his sister away from Longbourn. Elizabeth neither knew nor cared which was correct, and she was certain Miss Bingley had little chance of success either way. The gentlemen endured her for a few moments, then Mr. Bingley said something sharp. When Jane entered the room thereafter, he turned his attention to her. Then, when Mr. Darcy walked toward Elizabeth, Miss Bingley huffed and flung herself into a nearby chair, glaring at them all. What surprised Elizabeth most of all was how Mrs. Bennet watched, her gaze flinty with displeasure.

"Miss Elizabeth," greeted Mr. Darcy. "I hope you are well this fine day."

"I am," replied Elizabeth, for the briefest moment feeling satisfaction welling up within her for his civility to her and his hasty retreat from Miss Bingley. Then sanity set in, she remembered how much he exasperated her, and she schooled herself to the usual patience to endure him and waited for him to speak again.

"Did something pass between you and Miss Bingley before we entered the room?" asked he. "She was most insistent that we must return to Netherfield at once.

Elizabeth risked a glance at Miss Bingley, noting she appeared to be favoring them all with equal measures of her disdain. There was certainly nothing Elizabeth could do to further provoke her ire, so she put Miss Bingley from her mind.

"Nothing, in particular, Mr. Darcy. I have long understood that Miss Bingley did not care for myself, my family, and the neighborhood in general. Any scorn she sees fit to shower upon us will not affect me a jot, for I care not for her opinion."

Mr. Darcy gave her a sage nod. "That is for the best. I shall say nothing further, other than to confirm that you are correct to suspect her disinclination for you all. It is clear from your comments that I am not revealing anything unknown."

"Not at all," said Elizabeth, feeling herself softening toward this man.

For a moment he paused, looking at her, his manner as earnest as she had ever seen from him. That was saying much, of course, for she had always considered him an earnest sort of man, though one who was more prone to taciturnity.

"I have never admired her as she wishes, you know."

Elizabeth had not expected his comment, leading to her delayed reply. "I would never have thought it of you."

The gentleman's lips curled with mirth. "Have I been so open as to render my confession completely unsurprising? That is a shock, for I have always been told that I am very difficult to read."

"And I would agree with that assessment," replied Elizabeth. "But I have known of Miss Bingley's wishes as they pertain to you since the instant I made her acquaintance. While you are more difficult to understand, subsequent observation has allowed me to divine a hint of your feelings, and I dare say they are not to Miss Bingley's taste."

Mr. Darcy chuckled. "Then I shall need to be more circumspect, Miss Elizabeth, for I was not aware you were so adept at this business of observing your fellow men."

The gentleman paused and turned serious again. "While I have the opportunity, I should like to explain a little more of Mr. Wickham."

"It is unnecessary, Mr. Darcy," said Elizabeth. "I completely understand what sort of man he is, and I can only be ashamed of how my vaunted powers of observation utterly failed me." Elizabeth smiled at him and added: "Perhaps now you wish to take back your words from a few moments ago, for I have not proven myself nearly so adept as I supposed."

The look Mr. Darcy gave her could be called tender, though Elizabeth had never thought to ascribe such an adjective to him before. "It is a specialty of Wickham's, Miss Elizabeth, to portray himself in a manner not in keeping with his true character. If his efforts to mislead you succeeded, you are in good company, for he has done it all his life. My father, who was among the most intelligent and discerning men I have ever known, would hear nothing against him."

"And yet you knew he was not the man he portrayed himself to be?"

Mr. Darcy nodded. "I had an advantage my father never possessed. As I was near to him in age, I had the opportunity many times of seeing him in unguarded moments. Wickham would put a mask on when in company with my father, but that mask would often slip when he did not feel the need to be on his best behavior."

Elizabeth regarded the gentleman with some compassion. "That must have been hard, Mr. Darcy. Seeing your father so taken in could not have been welcome."

A sigh escaped the gentleman's lips. "It was difficult. After a time, however, I allowed the matter to rest, for I saw my father truly esteemed him and took joy from his presence." The man paused and gave her a wry grin. "As you must know, I am not the sort of man who can lighten others' moods by the force of my personality, yet Wickham was a man for whom such things came effortlessly. It was often my observation that my father had little joy in his life, especially after my mother passed; I did not wish to remove what joy he found in Wickham's company, even if I disapproved."

It was a sacrifice Elizabeth thought few men would make, and it improved her estimation of him. Perhaps he should have checked Mr. Wickham before now, but Elizabeth could not fault him for putting the needs of a beloved father before anything else. Mr. Darcy was a complex sort of man, such that a hasty judgment could not succeed in defining him. And suddenly Elizabeth realized she anticipated the opportunity to learn more of him, for he seemed eager to allow her that glimpse he had not before.

The sheer nearness of Miss Elizabeth's person, the force of her personality, the sensuality of every move, every word she spoke, was no less than intoxicating. And this when Darcy was convinced she still did not like him much! If he could ever persuade her to love him, to return his adoration in every particular, Darcy was uncertain he would survive the flames of her passion. There was no choice but to try, his aunt's machinations aside.

It left Darcy wondering how he could have thought to resist her allure. It was unfathomable. Regardless of what society thought of his decision, there could be no better woman for him, no brighter light in whose brilliance he could bask. He may as well have attempted to catch the sun in a bottle as search for some other woman who was her equal.

Incongruously Miss Bingley's eagerness to accost them the moment they entered the room had worked to his advantage and relief, even when Miss Elizabeth had spoken of the woman. It afforded Darcy the opportunity to gather himself, to prepare to meet and speak to her, to avoid being burned by the force of her personality. To avoid stammering and stuttering and looking the fool. While speaking of Wickham had not been precisely welcome, he knew she needed to know of the man, for it would play a vital part in the account he knew he would need to give her before she would ever accept his proposal.

The question was, how was she responding to him? Though Darcy watched her for any sign she was warming to him as she turned to other subjects, his observations remained inconclusive. Darcy had never been in doubt of her opinion of him before; perhaps it was more correct to say he had never thought a woman in her position would refuse a proposal from a man in his. How utterly insufficient his pretensions of pleasing a good woman had been! And he had not even been aware of his folly!

Darcy hoped this experience had made him a better man, a man she could come to esteem. To love. What he would do if he could not provoke her love he could not say. How could he ever live without it? Yet, he knew with a certainty that if she never offered him that boon, that sublimity of feeling, he would take whatever he could get from her. But persuading her to marry a man she did not love he thought would be near impossible. What a tangled web this was!

"Do you not think so, Mr. Darcy?"

Darcy blinked, suddenly aware the sound of her voice had spellbound him. Search his mind though he did, he could recall no memory of what she had said.

Seeing his consternation, Miss Elizabeth put a hand before her mouth and giggled. Giggled! Darcy had never seen such a thing from her. That she loved to laugh had been clear from the moment he met her, but she usually expressed her mirth with a low chuckle or a throaty laugh, sensual and warm. Evocative of her youngest sisters' silly merriment though it was, Darcy was charmed; it certainly did her no harm in his sight.

"I beg your pardon, Miss Elizabeth," said he, attempting to retrieve some measure of dignity, "but it appears I was not attending. Can I trouble you to repeat your question?"

This time she responded with her more customary warm laugh, melting his heart all over again. "Are you certain you wish me to repeat it?"

At that moment, Darcy knew she had been aware of his inattention for much longer than the few moments before her question. Trepidation coursed through him, but he gamely nodded and fixed her with a smile.

"It appears I was woolgathering longer than I thought. Did I make much of a fool of myself?"

"You agreed to some rather . . . interesting notions," said Miss Elizabeth, still chuckling and shaking her head. "You seemed to focus inward not long after we spoke of Mr. Wickham, but I knew you were not attending when I asked you a question that required a response, and you nodded your head. Since then, you agreed Lydia was the most beautiful of my sisters and the calmest and that we should run away to Gretna Green tomorrow."

Miss Elizabeth could not know how tempted he was to agree to that last, for Darcy immediately saw the benefits of just such an action. Refraining was difficult, but he smiled and pushed the matter to the back of his mind.

"Then perhaps I should answer the question you originally posed, and this time I will ensure that I attend."

"That will be impossible, for I do not remember it. It was a trifling matter, so there is no need for concern."

"Except for my incivility," said Darcy, bestowing a gaze on her that he hoped would feel full of warm regard. "There is no excuse; I promise to do better."

"It must have been something profound, sir," said she with an impish smile. "I might have thought you were contemplating the mysteries of the universe, so intent were you on your thoughts. Will you not share?"

There was little Darcy wished to do less than share the contents of his ruminations with her. It would not do to send her fleeing before he even had the chance to propose! Fortunately, a thought came to mind, a matter he had wanted to share with her, and one she would accept.

"Yes, there is a matter of which I would speak to you. I asked Bingley for permission to invite my sister to Netherfield, and being the excellent fellow he is, he agreed."

"That is excellent news, Mr. Darcy," said Miss Elizabeth. "But I have already heard of Miss Darcy's coming." Seeing Darcy's face fall, Miss Elizabeth hurried to assure him: "She will be very welcome here, I am sure."

It took no greatness of mind to determine who had spoken of Georgiana's coming. Darcy refrained from glaring at Miss Bingley, feeling a wave of irrational anger, as if she had stolen his news. It mattered little who told Miss Elizabeth—it was more important to ensure she welcomed the introduction.

"Then it appears Miss Bingley has anticipated me."

"That she has," replied Miss Elizabeth. "When is your sister to arrive?"

"Tomorrow. Colonel Fitzwilliam will escort her, and I suspect my cousin will find some means of persuading Bingley to allow him to stay for a time."

Miss Elizabeth gazed at him with mirth. "For a man of the scarlet, your cousin appears to do relatively little soldiering. I might have thought he would need to return to his regiment."

"That is what I have said frequently," replied Darcy. Then he sobered. "Fitzwilliam has been deployed to the continent and has returned to us safely. Though we tease him for his current inactivity, I know his mother worries that he will be deployed again."

"Yes, I can understand that," was her soft reply.

"Regardless, I do not mean to speak of my cousin," said Darcy, moving the conversation back to his sister. "When Georgiana comes, I have no doubt she will be delighted to be introduced to you and your family. With your permission, I shall bring her around at the first opportunity."

Miss Elizabeth's eyes shone first with surprise, then with pleasure. "Of course, Mr. Darcy. We would be happy to make Miss Darcy's acquaintance. Do you suppose you will come tomorrow?"

"I imagine we will. Fitzwilliam means to depart early enough to arrive for the midday meal. If it is no imposition, we shall come directly thereafter."

"It is no trouble at all," Miss Elizabeth assured him. "I shall inform my family. They will be eager to make her acquaintance." Miss Elizabeth paused and gave him a wry smile. "As I recall, Miss Bingley and Mrs. Hurst had much to say of your sister . . . ."

Miss Elizabeth trailed off, her brows drawing down in a frown. Darcy sensed she was not angry, but it appeared some unwelcome recollection had come over her.

"What is it, Miss Elizabeth?"

She paused for a long moment regarding him. After a moment she sighed and said: "Perhaps I should not say as much, but Miss Bingley implied in one of her letters to Jane that her brother admired your sister, and that an engagement would be soon forthcoming. I determined it was false, as your sister is still young as I understand, but I wonder at the audacity she displayed in speaking of it."

Darcy's eyes found Miss Bingley where she was sitting across the room near her brother and Miss Bennet. What she was doing he could not say, for he did not think she could have hope at this late date to keep her brother away from Miss Bennet. It appeared she did not believe it, for she was watching Darcy and Elizabeth closely, though he was certain she could not hear them. He might have thought she would join them, but at present, she appeared content to observe.

"I understand why she would say it," said Darcy to Miss Elizabeth, turning an apologetic smile on her. "It was a tool to discourage your sister, I suspect."

"That I determined for myself," said Miss Elizabeth with a tight grin.

"Yes, I can imagine you would. In all honesty, Miss Elizabeth, I have considered the possibility of Bingley marrying my sister. She is a shy girl, one lacking confidence, and I thought Bingley would do well for her. Of course, any such possibility depended on their attraction and her maturity. And I certainly never spoke to Miss Bingley on the subject, though I have long known that she wishes an alliance with Pemberley."

"That is not the only alliance she wishes," replied Miss Elizabeth with a laugh.

"As we have discussed before," agreed Darcy.

"Then will you not tell me more of your sister? I should love to hear about one I am to meet before long."

Until Darcy departed to return to Netherfield, they spent an agreeable time speaking of his sister. In Miss Elizabeth, he saw a determination to befriend her, and Darcy knew she would be an excellent friend for his sister. Even the youngest Miss Bennets, who were livelier than they should be, would assist Georgiana. Darcy felt his heart close to bursting yet again. Whereas Miss Bingley praised Georgiana to the skies, he knew it was all an attempt to impress him.

Miss Elizabeth would take her under her wing, nurture and guide her, teach her confidence, and provide true companionship. And she would become an even more important figure in Georgiana's life if Darcy could persuade Miss Elizabeth to marry him.

Never had the task seemed so daunting. But never had it seemed so attainable.

CHAPTER VI

"*D*earest Georgiana! How wonderful it is to see you again!"
As Miss Bingley's voice rang out across the entryway and echoed against the house, creating a dissonance of sound, Darcy reflected he had never noted how piercing her voice could be. Then again, there were many things about Miss Bingley he had never noticed before. It was equal parts inattention—for she had never interested him—and the woman being on her best behavior in his company. Now that she felt her ambitions slipping away from her, the control she exercised to restrain herself was slipping away, revealing more of the true person underneath.

To say that Darcy was not impressed was an understatement, for he was quickly coming to believe she was the sort of woman he had long detested. That she considered himself an excellent match was nothing more than a lack of self-awareness, and that without even considering her position in society relative to his. Darcy did not wish to think of the matter much, so he contented himself with the understanding he would not be happy with her and turned his attention to his sister.

Georgiana had always seen Miss Bingley's insincerity for what it was, her long-suffering endurance of the woman's ostentatious greeting obvious in the careful blankness with which she accepted the theatrics. For that matter, Bingley watched his sister, exasperation in his stance, as if he was considering interrupting her, for all it would be rude of him to do so. Bingley had not forgiven his sister for her reprehensible conduct toward Miss Bennet, rendering his patience less certain. Thus, Darcy stepped forward, partially to rescue his sister, but also to prevent an argument between his hosts.

"Georgiana," said he, stepping forward and accepting her embrace.

Miss Bingley's constant flow of words halted, and she looked at him with annoyance. Darcy had no trouble at all in ignoring her.

"And Fitzwilliam," said he, greeting his cousin when his sister pulled away. "Thank you for escorting Georgiana to Netherfield."

"It was no trouble, Darcy," said Fitzwilliam, grasping his shoulder in greeting. Then he turned to Bingley. "Thank you, Bingley, for agreeing to host me for a time. I have had little opportunity to be in my cousins' company of late, so your invitation is much appreciated."

"You may stay as long as you wish," said Bingley with a grin.

Miss Bingley, however, was not nearly so eager. "I have had rooms prepared for you both. But do your duties not recall you to your regiment soon?"

Fixing a delighted smirk on Miss Bingley, Fitzwilliam said: "No, I have no plans to return at present. I have some leave accumulated you see. And there are many events of great consequence afoot in Hertfordshire; I would not miss them if I can avoid it."

The smile with which Miss Bingley favored him became brittle. "You are welcome to stay, of course, though I cannot imagine what you mean. This is a dull location in a remote corner of the kingdom. There is nothing of interest here, and no one of any consequence."

"That is quite interesting, Miss Bingley," said Fitzwilliam. "And curious too. I have not been in the habit of considering a community not four hours from London, and not far from the Great North Road to be a 'remote corner of the kingdom.' What a curious statement."

"A little time here, and I have no doubt you will agree with me." Miss Bingley sniffed in disdain.

"Then I shall need to discover it for myself."

"Shall we not go inside?"

They all agreed and entered the house accompanied by Miss Bingley's statements concerning the house, how it was "barely adequate," yet seasoned with her self-congratulations at having done the best she could in assuring their comfort. Fitzwilliam engaged her at once, his look at Darcy suggesting Darcy concentrate on his sister.

Grateful for his interference, Darcy turned to Georgiana.

"Are you fatigued from your journey, Georgiana?"

"Not at all, Brother," replied his sister. "A little time in my room to refresh myself will set me right as rain."

"Then would you welcome a visit to a neighboring estate?"

It seemed Fitzwilliam had not been as successful in diverting Miss Bingley as he thought. "Oh, there is no need to go out again today, Mr. Darcy. I am certain your excellent sister would prefer to stay at Netherfield and rest."

"On the contrary," said Georgiana, "I believe I should like to meet your friends very much. If you will allow me a few moments to prepare, I shall join you directly."

"I shall show you to your room," said Darcy. "Fitzwilliam, will you not join us?"

It all happened so quickly that Miss Bingley appeared to be caught off guard. Any notion of her continued protestations ended when Bingley stepped forward to control her. As he climbed the stairs, Darcy glanced back, noting the woman's longing look, grateful for Bingley's actions.

"Forgive me if I speak out of turn, Darcy," said Fitzwilliam, "but I suspect that one will be trouble."

"I do not fear her." Darcy had not intended to be short with his cousin, but the comment carried that quality, regardless.

"Then you are a brave man, indeed."

"Brother," said Georgiana, drawing his attention back to her. "Are we to go to the home of the young lady you wrote about last year, about whom our cousin spoke much of the journey to Hertfordshire?"

"We are," said Darcy. "And I am eager to introduce you to her, for I believe she will become an excellent friend to you. She also has *four* sisters!"

As he might have expected, Georgiana betrayed a little trepidation at the notion and appeared as if she wished to say something further. A moment later, however, she nodded and excused herself, entering her room. Darcy walked with his cousin to the next room down the hall and ushered him in.

"What of Wickham?" asked Darcy without preamble.

After taking custody of Darcy's nemesis, Fitzwilliam had taken to the task of seeing to Wickham's disposition with almost unseemly eagerness. Yet, Darcy had heard nothing further, as Fitzwilliam had not written, unsurprising as it had not been long.

Fitzwilliam pulled his jacket from his frame and tossed it over the side of the chair, while his batman entered from the closet and set about assisting his commanding officer to change his clothes.

"We were lucky," said his cousin as he washed his face and hands. "There was a ship scheduled to depart for Van Diemen's Land yesterday. My brother, as you know, has no good opinion of Wickham, and was eager to remove him from British soil. He pulled a few strings and George Wickham, lately of His Majesty's militia, found himself on a ship bound for the very ends of the earth."

Fitzwilliam halted long enough to release a great guffaw. "I have never seen Wickham looking so poleaxed. I dare say he never expected to go from a windfall from our repulsive aunt to a prison ship bound for a penal colony in the space of a few days. You should have been there, Darcy, for it was as satisfying an experience as I have ever had."

"Good riddance," muttered Darcy. Then he eyed his cousin. "Did you discover how much Aunt Catherine paid him for his information?"

Fitzwilliam gave him an evil grin. "Much less than he wanted, to be certain, but Aunt Catherine has ever been miserly. Unless it relates to her food and clothing budget, of course. Let us simply say that Wickham had to settle for much less than he demanded."

"You have recovered that money?" When Fitzwilliam nodded, Darcy said: "I do not suppose there is any reason to return it to Aunt Catherine. Consider it a finder's fee and add it to whatever you are saving for your retirement."

"Thank you, Darcy," said Fitzwilliam, giving him a jaunty salute. "My brother said the same."

"I hope James knows to keep this matter to himself."

"Had I not intervened, I suspect he might have ridden to Rosings and taken our aunt over his knee. But I persuaded him that it was best to wait until our father returned to administer her chastisement."

Now fully dressed, Fitzwilliam thanked his batman, and the man departed from the room, leaving the cousins alone. "James will keep his peace for the moment. He also told me to inform you of his support for your efforts and his intention to attend the wedding, should it happen." Fitzwilliam grinned and added: "Are you making any progress on that front?"

"I believe Miss Elizabeth thinks better of me," replied Darcy. "But it is much too early to have captured her heart."

"Then you need to increase your efforts. Aunt Catherine will not wait long."

Darcy eschewed speaking in favor of nodding to his cousin, and they left the room. Georgiana had not yet emerged from her room, leaving the cousins to descend the stairs to await her arrival. This proved to be an unfortunate decision, for Miss Bingley was waiting in ambush, and pounced the moment their feet left the stairs.

"Mr. Darcy," said she, her countenance firm with determination, "I must beg you to reconsider this mad design to introduce your dear sister to the Bennet family. No good can come of exposing her to such an ill-mannered lot as they."

"I have met Miss Elizabeth and find her everything lovely," interjected Fitzwilliam. "And Miss Elizabeth has spoken of her family. Perhaps there are disparate characters among them, but any family of such a woman as she cannot be completely reprehensible."

"It appears she has duped you too, Colonel Fitzwilliam," said Miss Bingley, the sneer prominent in her voice. "There is nothing good in the woman, for she is a hoyden who cannot even measure up to the squalor in which she was raised."

"Is that so?" asked Fitzwilliam, his tone suggesting he was enjoying himself, while the diamond sparkling of his eyes suggested otherwise. "I apologize, Miss Bingley, for I had not heard that; I understood she was a gentlewoman. Has she naught but a tradesman for a father and she misled me?"

The granite set of Miss Bingley's jaw informed them both that she understood Fitzwilliam's reference very well. She paused a moment to gather her composure, allowing Darcy to speak before she could.

"I have no compunction at all about introducing Georgiana to the Bennets, Miss Bingley. She will, I am certain, be eager to meet young ladies her age."

"Before you say anything further, I suggest you think better of it, Caroline."

Bingley strode toward them with purpose, his unfriendly glare fixed on his sister. "It would be best if you minded your own concerns. You can have nothing to say about Miss Darcy's acquaintances. If you disagree, you may stay home."

That was not palatable to Miss Bingley, for while she hated Longbourn and its inhabitants, she understood the danger by now and did not wish to leave Darcy in Miss Elizabeth's company. Thus, she subsided, though not without a hateful glare at her brother. Georgiana descended soon, and they entered the carriage for the brief journey to Netherfield. Darcy was grateful Bingley had possessed the foresight to call for his carriage in addition to Darcy's own, for he did not wish to share a confined space with an angry Miss Bingley.

*   *   *

"Miss Elizabeth, how fortunate I am to be in your company again."

As Elizabeth greeted Colonel Fitzwilliam with pleasure, she did not overlook Miss Bingley's snort of disagreement, a singularly unladylike reaction. Colonel Fitzwilliam, as a truly well-bred man, ignored the woman's incivility and gestured to a young lady who had entered with Mr. Darcy.

"If you introduce me to your family, I will reciprocate and introduce my cousin to your acquaintance."

"As I am already acquainted with the Bennets," said Mr. Darcy, "perhaps I should handle the introductions."

"Nonsense, Darcy," said Colonel Fitzwilliam. "I am far more jovial than you are. I am certain the Bennets would be more than happy to allow me to speak."

"Oh, we esteem Mr. Darcy very much," said Mrs. Bennet. "He is everything gentlemanly and good."

Colonel Fitzwilliam turned an upraised eyebrow on his cousin. "Is that so? Well, Darcy, it appears you have acquired a hint of civility in your manner."

"Anthony!" scolded the young woman. "If you persist, I shall never be introduced to these people!"

Had Elizabeth not been watching, she might have missed it, for Mr. Darcy and his cousin shared a look Elizabeth could not quite interpret but seemed laced with meaning. Elizabeth offered the introductions, then the colonel responded in kind as he had designed. Then a curious thing happened, for Miss Darcy appeared to shrink in on herself, as if the notion of meeting the Bennets, which she had demanded only a moment before, was now the most daunting task.

"Welcome to our home, Miss Darcy," said Elizabeth, eager to put the girl at ease. "We are thrilled to make your acquaintance."

As Elizabeth spoke to her and led her to a nearby sofa with her brother in attendance, she noted how Kitty and Lydia could not wait to pounce on Colonel Fitzwilliam.

"Is it true you are a colonel?" asked Lydia, Kitty looking on with widened eyes.

"It is, Miss Lydia," replied Colonel Fitzwilliam with aplomb.

"How wonderful!" exclaimed Kitty. "We know only one other colonel, and he is stuffy and old!"

Colonel Fitzwilliam did not restrain his hilarity, guffawing at her statement. Kitty appeared to understand she had spoken out of turn, for she reddened with embarrassment. But the colonel spoke to her kindly, saying:

"I dare say some officers are stuffy, indeed! Why, I once knew a general who would not speak unless to say something that would put his men to sleep.

"But you should know, Miss Kitty, Miss Lydia," continued he with marked enjoyment, "that this colonel of whom you speak is naught but a militia officer. I, on the other hand, am an officer in the cavalry and have seen battle against the French."

This seemed to impress the girls, for they clamored for him to tell them stories of his exploits, to which he agreed without hesitation. They led him to a sofa where he regaled them with his tales of danger and romance, and if Mrs. Bennet leaned forward and listened with as much interest as her daughters, Elizabeth could not blame her, for Colonel Fitzwilliam was an agreeable man.

"I am happy to make your acquaintance at last, Miss Elizabeth," said Miss Darcy, pulling Elizabeth's attention to her.

"'At last?'" echoed Elizabeth.

"Well," said the girl, seeming to think she had spoken out of turn by the sudden duck of her head, "my brother and cousin have spoken of you, and my brother mentioned you in his letters to me in the autumn."

Miss Bingley gasped, her accusing eyes finding Mr. Darcy. Elizabeth, however, had no attention for anyone other than the gentleman and his sister. With deliberate slowness, she quirked an eyebrow at the gentleman, and said to his sister:

"Then I must wonder at your desire to meet me, for Mr. Darcy has ever been my fiercest critic!"

"Oh, not at all!" exclaimed Miss Darcy, her eyes flying to Elizabeth's face. Then she seemed to catch something of Elizabeth's humor, for she smiled, though uncertainly. "Not at all."

"I might not have thought I warranted enough of your interest to mention me to your sister, sir."

Elizabeth injected a challenge into her tone, and the gentleman did not hesitate to accept it. "If you recall, we engaged in some rather . . . spirited discussions, especially when you stayed at Netherfield. I recounted a few instances in my letters."

Elizabeth considered the man. "I do recall you writing a letter one evening when we were in company."

"Yes, that was one such occasion," agreed Mr. Darcy. "Considering our conversation while I was attempting to write, you can hardly suppose I would not make any mention of it."

"That is understandable, I suppose."

While the man's assertion was believable—and Miss Bingley wished to believe it, as she sagged in relief—Elizabeth could not help but feel he had left something out. There was little enough reason to belabor the point, however, so she turned back to Miss Darcy.

Had Miss Bingley not been present, Elizabeth thought the ensuing conversation might have been engaging, for Miss Darcy was a sweet girl, though as shy as any she had ever met. But Miss Bingley appeared intent on preventing them, for she interjected her opinion at every opportunity, disrupting their conversation with her observations. Had she had much of interest to say, she might have added to their discourse, but much of what she said consisted of veiled insults, innuendo, and her continual attempts to contradict whatever Elizabeth said. Within a few moments, Elizabeth was glaring at the woman. Mr. Darcy, and even Miss Darcy, appeared exasperated with her.

An alteration of the company saw an increase in Miss Darcy's easiness, for, after a time of telling them stories, Colonel Fitzwilliam turned more of his attention on Mr. Bennet. That was when Kitty and Lydia, unsurprisingly, made their wish for Georgiana's company known, leading to her position between them. For all that Kitty and Lydia carried the conversation, a few moments' observation informed Elizabeth that the girl was easier out of Miss Bingley's company, and though still reserved, chatted amiably with Elizabeth's younger sisters.

Miss Bingley was not a proponent of the changed circumstances if her glower at the three was any indication. This contained a hidden benefit, for it distracted her, allowing Elizabeth to speak with Mr. Darcy without her interference.

"What a lovely girl your sister is, Mr. Darcy," said she, pulling the gentleman's attention back to her. Elizabeth paused, uncertain if she should speak the thought that came to mind. Then she shook her hesitation aside and said: "Thus, the last of Mr. Wickham's falsehoods is laid bare."

Mr. Darcy gave her a sharp look. "Wickham spoke of my sister?"

Elizabeth thought the man wished to retrieve his enemy and administer a little extra retribution. Seeing his anger, Elizabeth hastened to say:

"Only briefly and only to say that she was proud."

While Elizabeth could readily see the gentleman was not amused, he shook it off. "Yes, I can imagine that is the least of what Wickham would say, for he has no compunction about spreading lies wherever he goes."

"Yes, that much is beyond dispute," murmured Elizabeth. She regarded the man by her side. "If I might be so bold, I hope whatever action you have taken against Mr. Wickham will render him unable to prey upon others again."

"I should have taken action against him years ago," said Mr. Darcy, and Elizabeth could see how regretful he was. "But you need have no further concern for him, for he is now gone, and shall not return."

Such a statement was likely to mean a penal colony, and while such an existence could not be agreeable, Elizabeth had heard enough of Mr. Wickham's deeds to know that was where he belonged. Elizabeth gave the gentleman her agreement and determined to drop the subject.

"I would like to thank you and your family for accepting my sister with such a warm welcome," said Mr. Darcy. "As you must have noted, Georgiana is a shy girl, one who does not make friends easily." Mr. Darcy fixed her with a self-deprecating smile. "In many respects, she is easily recognizable as my sister, for we share many of the same traits. They are traits long associated with my family."

"Then my sisters must be a shock to her," said Elizabeth, suppressing her mirth. "Under no circumstances could we call Lydia and Kitty 'shy.' Far too bold for their own good would be much nearer the mark, I should think."

"There is something to be said for confidence. Georgiana could do with a liberal dose of it."

"That is interesting, Mr. Darcy," said Elizabeth, "for I see no lack of confidence in you."

Mr. Darcy chuckled and acknowledged her point. "No, I have never borne that cross. My reserve differs greatly from my sister's. I can only think that an association with two such assertive girls can only be to her benefit."

"And yet you may wish to take care," replied Elizabeth. When he regarded her, she gave him a soft smile. "I am not blind to my family's faults, Mr. Darcy. My youngest sisters are far too forward. While I cannot imagine they will influence your sister away from her good behavior, it would be best to be watchful."

Mr. Darcy considered them, and Elizabeth thought she could see the memories of the ball at Netherfield, Kitty and Lydia running amok, laughing with abandon and forgetting any measure of restraint in his eyes. When he did not speak at once, Elizabeth wondered what he was thinking, for surely, to a man so accustomed to the best society could offer, their behavior was nothing less than reprehensible.

"Yes, I agree sometimes your sisters could benefit from a dose of more proper behavior," said Mr. Darcy.

"But?" prompted Elizabeth when he did not continue at once.

Mr. Darcy sighed and gave her a wry smile. "I have often thought, in my sister's case, that a hint of extra confidence would not go amiss. Sometimes I have thought your sisters could use the opposite, yet I would not preach to you on the subject; you are more than intelligent enough to know when boldness is required, and when caution should reign."

"I do," confirmed Elizabeth.

"Then let us hope our sisters will each share their qualities so they may improve in those things they lack."

Elizabeth regarded him for a long moment. "I must own, Mr. Darcy, that it has not been long since I thought you would never wish your sister to mingle with mine."

"And you would not have been incorrect then," said the gentleman with no hint of hesitation. "But I like to think I have learned in the interim. Or perhaps it is more correct to say that I have *remembered*."

It was a curious statement, and one Elizabeth wished to clarify. At that moment, however, Miss Bingley approached and pushed the matter from Elizabeth's mind. She was unhappy, striving to ignore Elizabeth as she focused on the gentleman.

"Mr. Darcy, I believe you must look to your sister." With a disdainful glare at Elizabeth, she added: "If you do not rescue her at once, they will corrupt her beyond all redemption!"

Elizabeth followed the gentleman's gaze to the three girls and was pleased to note how their heads were together, how they laughed, though much more quietly than Kitty and Lydia's usual loud merriment. Allowing her gaze to roam back and forth between the three girls and Miss Bingley, Elizabeth could not quite determine what had offended her. By Mr. Darcy's confused expression, she knew he was in the same predicament.

"I cannot understand your meaning, Miss Bingley," said he. "It appears to me they are getting on famously."

"Has this entire improper family tainted you too?" demanded she. "Look at them! Do you not see the raucous laughter into which they have dragged her?"

"Upon my word!" exclaimed Elizabeth, no longer able to remain silent. "By this account, Miss Bingley, you must be a Puritan, opposed to *all* laughter. They appear remarkably restrained to me."

Miss Bingley turned a baleful glare on Elizabeth, but Mr. Darcy spoke to forestall her vitriol. "Miss Elizabeth is correct. I see nothing the matter with their behavior."

"Mr. Darcy!"

"Please, Miss Bingley," replied he, censure in his voice, "allow me the discernment to know when my ward is not behaving as she ought. It is none of your concern, so I advise you to drop the subject."

For a moment Miss Bingley did not know how to respond. Then she flounced away in a huff, throwing herself into a nearby chair and glaring at them all. The way Mrs. Bennet watched her, unfriendliness etched on every line of her face, Elizabeth could see her mother had heard some of what Miss Bingley said and did not appreciate the woman's conceit. Mercifully, however, she restrained her impulse to respond and remained content with her glower.

There Miss Bingley stayed for the rest of the visit, and no one appeared to repine her discourtesy. Elizabeth ignored the woman, for she was much better engaged speaking with Mr. Darcy.

CHAPTER VII

"*I* have a letter from my father."

Darcy looked at his cousin with interest. "It cannot be a response to the express you sent him, for it is much too soon."

"That it is," agreed Fitzwilliam. "But it is interesting nonetheless."

"Oh?" asked Darcy.

"You may read it for yourself," said Fitzwilliam, gesturing with the letter, "but the gist of it is that Father has finished managing the problem at the estate in County Cork and means to hurry home. While he gives me no details, he speaks of a letter he received from Lady Catherine that has concerned him. It appears she wrote to him of the impending engagement between her daughter and nephew."

Darcy fixed his cousin with a sharp look. "Do you imply that Lady Catherine wrote to the earl of the information she thought to use against me?"

Fitzwilliam demurred. "Again, my father was not explicit, but I expect that is exactly what she did."

At his cousin's offer, Darcy took the missive and perused it. As Fitzwilliam informed him, the earl said nothing openly, likely because he did not wish to do so in an unsecured letter. However, from his language, it was clear his sister's letter had angered him, his hurried return from Ireland calculated to ensure she did not make a grave mistake.

"When did your father send this," asked Darcy, looking for a postmark. As there was none, he glanced at the top of the letter, noting it was dated a week earlier

Fitzwilliam nodded. "Father sent it in the care of a trusted footman. After he crossed the Irish Sea, the footman made his way south as quickly as he could. When he arrived at the house in town, another servant took the letter and brought it here."

"Then he may not arrive in time to deal with Lady Catherine," said Darcy with a grimace.

"He may not," said Fitzwilliam.

"But Lady Catherine has yet to reveal her plans, so we cannot say with any certainty. She may yet wait long enough."

"That is an extraordinary hope, Darcy," said Fitzwilliam. "The longer I think of this mess, the more inclined I am to believe you may be acting precipitously. If you refuse to marry Anne, what does it matter if you are already married to Miss Elizabeth or still single? I should think Lady Catherine would respond the same, regardless."

Darcy considered his cousin's argument and shook his head after a moment. "In the end, I cannot believe that Lady Catherine wishes to bring infamy on the family. There is a greater chance she will desist if there is no more prospect of my marrying Anne."

"If you ask me," said Fitzwilliam, a hint of hilarity rising in his voice, "I believe you simply wish to use the excuse to prompt Miss Elizabeth to accept you."

There was no denying that was a facet of Darcy's thinking, though he did not wish his cousin to know that. "While I will not deny that I believe Miss Elizabeth will greatly increase my happiness if I can convince her, chief among my thoughts is the need to protect Georgiana and the family name."

"Then that is understandable. Fortunately, my father is a liberal man, else he might become angry at your choice of a bride. The only worse choice in society's eyes among your acquaintances is Miss Bingley, little chance though there is that she will ever realize her wishes."

Darcy shuddered, much to his cousin's amusement. Marrying Miss Bingley was not an option, especially not given what Darcy had learned of her character these past weeks. If Miss Bingley was his only recourse, Darcy would have preferred to refuse Lady Catherine's demands and brave whatever the ton had to say, and he knew Georgiana would have agreed with his assessment. She wished to have Miss Bingley for a sister as little as Darcy wished her for his wife.

Underneath it, however, Darcy confronted the truth of his cousin's words, that he wished to take advantage of the situation to secure a woman who, by all accounts, disliked him. Then again, the warmth he had seen from her these previous days was not his imagination. Darcy did not fool himself into thinking that she was deeply in love with him, for the falsehood of such a belief was impossible to refute. But had her opinion changed enough to allow him to propose? Unfortunately, Darcy did not think Lady Catherine would allow him the time he would need to make that determination.

"It has been my observation," said Fitzwilliam, pulling Darcy from his introspection, "that she is softening toward you."

"You have echoed my thoughts precisely," replied Darcy with an absence of mind.

"Then it would behoove you to move quickly, Darcy. Lady Catherine will have you shackled to Anne otherwise."

"Did you not just accuse me of using the opportunity to force Miss Elizabeth into matrimony?"

Fitzwilliam laughed and shook his head. "Perhaps I did. While I am not certain you are correct about Lady Catherine's restraint, I do not dispute your convictions. The question is, can you convince her?"

"I am trying."

The cousins allowed their mirth free rein, Darcy reflecting on what an excellent man to have as a supporter. This would all be much more difficult if Fitzwilliam was not the man he was.

"How long can you stay?" asked Darcy, the thought he would not welcome his cousin's departure making itself known.

"I am at your disposal," replied Fitzwilliam. "There is no need to return to my post, and my general has given me extended leave." Fitzwilliam paused to scratch his nose. "In truth, I suspect I might like the taste of freedom so much that it will lead me to retire."

Darcy regarded his cousin with interest. "What of your intention to remain in the army until the war is over? You will not receive half pay if you leave early."

"That is true," acknowledged Fitzwilliam. "At the same time, I do not relish the possibility of returning to the battlefront again, and there are rumors of my regiment's imminent dispatch to the continent. The joy of dodging bullets has lost its charm."

"Your mother will be pleased," observed Darcy. "And your father has all but promised he would see you receive an estate."

"There is one not far from Pemberley that may be left to me," said Fitzwilliam.

"Thorndell," said Darcy with a nod.

"But old Connolly does not appear willing to give up the ghost just yet." Fitzwilliam chuckled. "It may be many years before he makes way for me to inherit."

"Until then, your father is eager to support you, and your mother would badger him if he was not. There are few reasons to return, and every reason to retire."

"That is what I think. This interlude in the country will give me time to consider my future; Rosings is not conducive to such reflection, as I am certain you will agree."

"Why would I disagree with so incontrovertible a fact?" asked Darcy.

"Why, indeed," murmured Fitzwilliam. Then he turned to regard Darcy frankly. "There is an added benefit, you know. With my presence, you will have another to help keep Miss Bingley from you. Given what I have seen of the lady, it may take a battalion. But I shall do my best."

It was not a matter about which to laugh. It was a distraction and irritation that Darcy did not need. But he thanked his cousin, and they turned to other subjects.

Miss Caroline Bingley pulled away from the door through which she had been listening, incensed with the oafish Colonel Fitzwilliam for how he had insulted her. For a moment, she thought to enter the room and deliver a stinging set down to the odious man for daring to speak of her in such a way.

While Caroline was too angry to see it for the moment, it was fortunate that she had refrained. One did not act in such a manner toward a man who was the son of a peer. All Caroline could think about was her offense and what she meant to do about it, for there was no question of allowing this outrage to stand.

And Mr. Darcy! He for whom she had possessed so much hope, to speak of her in such a way, if only to his cousin! Caroline could only wonder what he could be thinking. How could any man of discernment consider impertinent Miss Eliza Bennet superior to her? It was unfathomable.

The fears she had espoused since they had first come to this forsaken place had come to pass, it seemed, for if she did not do something quickly, Mr. Darcy would be lost to her. There were many things of which they had spoken that confused Caroline, for she could not imagine why Mr. Darcy needed to marry at once. And there was a nagging sensation that had she happened upon their conversation only a few moments earlier, she would have learned the truth of the matter. It seemed centered on his aunt. But knowing of Lady Catherine de Bough's insistence regarding her daughter, she knew the lady would be of no assistance. If the man needed to marry with such haste, Caroline would accept him this very instant—they could be married tomorrow. And yet, he fixed his hopes on that chit Eliza Bennet! It was nigh unbelievable.

When she reached the sanctuary of her room, Caroline stalked inside, ready to put her hands on something—anything—that would allow her to vent her anger. She eyed the delicate porcelain figurines on the mantle but restrained herself with an effort. While the sight of shattering glass might satisfy her for the moment, she knew it would turn to regret at once, for many of those pieces had been gifts from her mother. Denied an immediate release, Caroline took to pacing the room.

But no relief came to mind, for she did not know what she could do. A compromise was out of the question, for Caroline was not a woman to stoop to such underhanded means, and even if she succeeded, she could not be sure he would not refuse. A niggling thought tickled the back of her mind, the memory of Mr. Darcy speaking to the detestable Miss Eliza, confessing to the possession of an implacable temper. He was such a man that Caroline could not imagine the possibility of his mistreatment of anyone. But it was an established fact that a man possessed the power over a wife to make her life miserable, and Caroline did not wish to test the theory. Better that he came to her, for that would give her a certain measure of power in a marriage.

Had Caroline been of a mind, she might have spent the afternoon in furious contemplation, exasperating herself against Mr. Darcy and his blindness. A burst of energy could not last indefinitely, however, and at length, Caroline tired of her pacing. Unwilling to remain in her room while Mr. Darcy dreamed of making love to the chit, she made her way below stairs to the sitting-room, where she came across Georgiana Darcy.

A hint of a plan formed in her mind upon seeing the girl there. Mr. Darcy was a man full-grown, more than a decade his sister's elder, rendering her opinion in the matter less influential than Caroline might have hoped. But surely, he would not discount her opinion entirely. If Caroline could move the girl to her support, perhaps she might yet salvage the situation.

"Good morning, Georgiana," greeted Caroline, watching as the girl looked up. There was something in her look, something on which Caroline could not quite put her finger. But she did not like the look of it. She did not like it at all.

"I apologize for leaving you alone this morning," said she as she moved to join Georgiana on the sofa. "Several matters prevented me from attending you."

"It is no trouble, Miss Bingley," said Miss Darcy.

Caroline had a distinct impression that the girl held herself a little more erect than was her custom, and it was not so much her physical posture as a perception of her confidence. That was not to Caroline's taste, for a mousey, uncertain Georgiana better suited her purposes. Yet there was nothing to be done, so Caroline forged ahead.

"I am uncertain where the gentlemen are this morning, but I am entirely at your disposal. Shall we play the pianoforte together?"

"While I am pleased to do so, it will need to wait for another time." When Caroline regarded her with confusion, Miss Darcy stated: "Yesterday, during our visit to Longbourn, I agreed to meet the Bennet sisters in Meryton this morning. We shall leave in a quarter of an hour."

Caroline could not prevent her countenance from falling at the news. "'We?'"

"My brother and my cousin are to go," replied Georgiana, apparently unconcerned with Caroline's annoyance. "I cannot say if your brother will accompany us, but considering his interest in Miss Bennet, it will surprise me if he does not."

Displeasure again rose in Caroline's breast like bile, stinging her heart with the sharpness of thrusting needles. "Georgiana, dearest, I believe it may be best if you abjured the Bennet sisters. They are not of your sphere, and their behavior is the sort you would not wish to emulate."

Georgiana regarded her, no trace of the timid little girl she had been the last time Caroline had been in her company. Could she have changed so much in a matter of a few months?

"You do not care for the Bennets."

The snort that came to Caroline's lips was not ladylike, and she avoided releasing it by the barest of margins. "I cannot understand any other opinion. They are an uncouth family, with characters unworthy of the title of gentlefolk. If you had seen what I have, you would not be so quick to befriend them."

"And yet my brother has recommended them to me with a measure of approval I cannot misunderstand."

"*Miss Eliza Bennet* has taken your brother in!"

Had Caroline understood how she appeared when she spat the name from her lips like rancid cream, she might have refrained. What she *did* notice was how Georgiana's expression became stony with displeasure; she had never seen as much from the diffident girl.

"She has not taken William in, Miss Bingley," said Georgiana. "I apologize if it offends you, but I suspect Miss Elizabeth will one day be my sister."

"No!" breathed Caroline, horrified that even this tenuous avenue to Mr. Darcy seemed closed.

"I do," affirmed the girl. "Though I have known her for only one day, I cannot but think William has made a wise choice. I have no intention of offending, yet at the same time, I must inform you that my brother never intended to offer for you. How much sorrow it causes to hear it, I cannot say, but it is the truth, and you had best understand it.

"Remember that my brother is a man in command of his future and may do as he pleases. I apologize again if I cause you grief, but I will not lie to you. This hope of yours is doomed, for there was never any chance of his proposing to you."

For the first time since she had been a girl, Caroline had no notion of what she should say. How her plans could have gone so awry was beyond her ability to comprehend. It was perhaps fortunate that the door opened, and Colonel Fitzwilliam looked into the room. His countenance as he regarded them appeared wary, and Caroline realized with a start that Mr. Darcy had often looked at her with the same expression, especially of late.

"Miss Bingley, Georgiana," said he, stepping into the room. "The carriage waits on the drive for our excursion." Then he turned his attention to Caroline. "My apologies, Miss Bingley, but I do not know if you intend to accompany us to meet the Bennets in Meryton?"

In answer to his question, Caroline found herself shaking her head, unable to muster even a single word. Colonel Fitzwilliam nodded and extended his hand to Georgiana, who took it with apparent relief. They said their farewells and departed, though Caroline heard not a word. Instead, she sat staring at the door through which they had disappeared, unable to summon anything to mind, aware of only one fact. It was a hopeless business. She, Caroline Bingley, had failed when she had been so certain of success. Yet confessing defeat was unthinkable.

As the carriage approached the little town of which her new friends had spoken with such fondness, Georgiana Darcy's mind was focused on other matters. Miss Bingley's attempt had not been a surprise, for she had expected it from the moment she entered the house; as a point of fact, the woman had already tried a version of it, little though Georgiana could understand how she thought she might find success.

Georgiana had never liked Caroline, for in her manners she had always seen a grasping woman, one who looked on little Georgiana Darcy as a means to burrow her way into her brother's life. It had often been thus. It was difficult to comprehend why such predatory women thought she was a senseless ninny, but she had seen it too many times to question it.

That was why Miss Elizabeth Bennet had been such a breath of fresh air. Georgiana had spent only a short time with her the previous day, but it had been enough to inform her that Miss Elizabeth was genuine, a woman not interested in such paltry devices. William had not told her directly that he meant to make Miss Elizabeth an offer, but Georgiana knew his ways, understood his esteem for her through observation. And she had a distinct impression that Miss Elizabeth would make a wonderful sister. While her new acquaintance with Kitty and Lydia dominated Georgiana's current attention, she was certain her relationship with Miss Elizabeth would eventually be much closer, even if she did not become Georgiana's sister.

As the carriage rolled into town, Georgiana formed a resolution. She had avoided all her brother and cousin's questions, Mr. Bingley looking on, understanding his sister's character, as she did not think it signified. But before she could allow herself to concentrate her attention on her new friends, she wished to speak with Miss Elizabeth.

When her brother handed her from the coach, she greeted her friends with excitement, never having had many girls her age with whom to associate. The youngest Bennets did not accept her stated desire for Miss Elizabeth's company with any equanimity, prompting Georgiana to hasten to reassure them.

"I have something of which I wish to speak to her. But I shall join you directly."

Thus, when the party turned to the town, Georgiana put herself in Miss Elizabeth's company, and turned to her, intending to speak at once.

"I would not presume to suggest you are not aware of Miss Bingley's character, Miss Elizabeth, but I should like to inform you of a conversation between us this morning."

Miss Elizabeth looked at her, puzzled and suspicious all at once. "I cannot imagine what Miss Bingley would have to say of *me*. I can scarcely think of two people with less in common and less to say to each other."

It was impossible to hold her mirth in, leading her to take Miss Elizabeth's arm to hide her chuckles. "Perhaps you would be correct if you suggested there is little for you to say *to* each other. But Miss Bingley has no hesitation at all about speaking *of* you."

"Yes, I suppose I should have suspected it," said Miss Elizabeth, her grimace telling the story of her feelings for the other woman. "I cannot suppose any of it was good."

"You appear to know her well," replied Georgiana. "Forgive me if I speak out of turn, Miss Elizabeth, but I would have you know my feelings."

"Your feelings?"

"Of you and William."

For a moment, the woman appeared puzzled. Then her eyes darted to Georgiana's brother, who stood with Anthony a short distance from them, and then returned to her with a hint of demand.

"Do not suppose my brother has confided in me, for he has not. But I know him, Miss Elizabeth. He would not be so open in his admiration if he did not mean to do something about it. William does not need my approval, nor would I hesitate to give it to him should he ask. But I wish you to know right now that I approve."

Shock stained Miss Elizabeth's face, such that she could not respond at once. When she did, her thoughts went in a different direction from what Georgiana had expected.

"What does this have to do with Miss Bingley?"

Georgiana regarded her new friend, wondering at how she avoided the primary topic. But she was not at all opposed to answering.

"Why, only that Miss Bingley considers herself the best choice to become my brother's wife. She has not hesitated to inform me of her opinion of your family and how you are not suitable acquaintances."

Miss Elizabeth's gaze turned flinty. "I suppose that we, being gentlefolk, are not good enough for the daughter of a tradesman."

Again, Georgiana giggled. "Except she does not see it that way. But yes, you have the gist of her feelings.

"The important part I wish you to understand is that I have never liked Miss Bingley. There has always been something artful in her air that put me on my guard. I have never wished to have her for a sister, and William has never considered offering for her."

"Yet you believe he will offer for me."

Georgiana regarded her, wondering at her manner. Her regard for her brother was such that she could not imagine any woman greeting the prospect of his attention with anything other than giddy excitement, yet Miss Elizabeth's response was even, perhaps a little taken aback. It was not a matter she wished to consider at any length, for she trusted her brother to manage the situation between them. Her only purpose that day was to ensure Miss Elizabeth understood her approbation.

"I know my brother," was Georgiana's simple reply. "Now, if you will excuse me, I believe your sisters are waiting impatiently for my return. Unless I am much mistaken, my brother is scarcely less eager for your company."

With those last words, Georgiana squeezed Miss Elizabeth's hand and approached Kitty and Lydia. While they looked at her, questions floating in their eyes, they said nothing, guiding her away toward the milliner's. Georgiana went willingly, allowing them to immerse her in their chatter. If she could not force herself to be quite so voluble as they, the warmth of their friendship still filled her heart, leading her to openness of which she might not have thought herself capable. Yielding to their persuasion, she joined them with a will.

CHAPTER VIII

"*M*iss Elizabeth, shall we?"

Drawn from her contemplation of Georgiana Darcy, Elizabeth turned to note Mr. Darcy watching her, his arm extended. For the briefest moment, Elizabeth could not respond, for the words this man's sister had spoken to her still echoed in her mind. Did Mr. Darcy have any knowledge of what she meant to say? If so, what was she to do about it?

Finding the ability to respond deep within herself, Elizabeth smiled and accepted, resting her hand on his jacket lightly, as if any further imprint upon the fabric would signify some commitment she was unprepared to make. Conversation between them did not flow, for Elizabeth could not break the hold Miss Darcy's words had over her, and Mr. Darcy appeared to sense she was considering something at length.

Could she be mistaken? It was possible, Elizabeth supposed, though she had noted the gentleman's actions since her return to Hertfordshire. Then she also had Charlotte's oft-stated opinion of Mr. Darcy's interest to consider. Elizabeth had not given her friend's repeated statements much credence, but now Elizabeth could only be amazed by how accurate her friend's assertions had been. She had been more observant than Elizabeth had been herself.

"Miss Elizabeth?"

Interrupted, Elizabeth turned to regard Mr. Darcy, who was watching her with some concern. Then she noted how his eyes found his sister, more than a hint of exasperation contained therein.

"Did my sister say something to upset you, Miss Elizabeth?" asked he, turning again to face her.

"Of course not, Mr. Darcy," said Elizabeth, summoning a smile for his benefit. "Miss Darcy is everything lovely and, I suspect, incapable of giving offense. I apologize for my distraction; you now have my attention."

Mr. Darcy regarded her, doubt etched upon his countenance. After a moment, he nodded, and they turned back to the street. The ensuing conversation remained banal, little of any importance passing between them other than observations of the shops they passed, or the number of redcoats gathered on the streets. Now that Mr. Wickham was not among their number, Elizabeth could not help but suppose the officers little interested the gentleman. While they were thus engaged, Elizabeth formed a resolution of obtaining some little measure of that knowledge she did not yet possess about the gentleman's intentions.

"It was a surprise to learn of your visit to my aunt's house in London," said she as they were watching the girls look over bits of ribbon in the haberdashers.

"I found your aunt and uncle to be excellent people," replied he, a hint of a smile indicating his approval. "And I might never have suspected us of having a connection through nearby residences."

"Yes, I suppose it must have been," said Elizabeth. "My aunt has often spoken of Derbyshire and her time there, though I do not remember her mentioning a name."

"The name of the town would have meant nothing to you," said Mr. Darcy.

"That is true," said Elizabeth. She paused, wondering what she should say, then ventured: "Yet, I seem to remember a time when the thought of visiting a neighborhood such as Cheapside was not palatable."

A frown covered the gentleman's face. "You have my apologies, Miss Elizabeth, but I do not recall a time when we spoke of your uncle's place of residence."

"As I recall, Miss Bingley made it clear when she delayed the return visit to my sister for three weeks."

"And her brother has spoken to her harshly on that subject." Mr.

Darcy regarded her. "Are you equating my opinion of the locale to Miss Bingley's?"

"Were you in ignorance of my sister's presence?" rejoined Elizabeth.

The gentleman smiled. "Do you not know it is impolite to answer a question with a question?"

Elizabeth did not respond, keeping her attention fixed on the gentleman, who chuckled and responded: "Yes, Miss Elizabeth, I was aware of your sister's presence in London. I knew of her visit to Miss Bingley, for the woman herself informed me of it. However, I will point out that I knew nothing of Miss Bingley's maneuvering, and I would have counseled against such an obvious display of contempt for another had I known."

For a long moment, Elizabeth regarded him, feeling a hint of surprise at his open acknowledgment of his actions. "Why did you keep it from him?"

Mr. Darcy sighed and raked a hand through his hair. "From the mistaken assumption about your sister's response to his interest."

Elizabeth frowned. "What do you mean?"

"It was my opinion that she did not favor him, that your mother might insist she accept any overtures he might make."

Offense soared in Elizabeth's breast, but before she could speak any of the dozen retorts that came into her mind, he spoke first.

"I know what you will say, and I cannot but agree with you. It was a mistake, and one I have since confessed to my friend. At the same time, I will assert that your sister's manner is not one to invite an easy comprehension of her feelings, for she is nearly as reticent as I am myself."

"You should not have presumed to judge!" snapped Elizabeth. "It was more than a little officious on your part."

Mr. Darcy nodded readily, though his action was not one of complacency. "It is a valuable lesson, for I have learned that I am not qualified to advise on matters of the heart. Bingley is an excellent fellow and has forgiven me. Your sister has also extended the same balm, though she has not spoken the words. I know it because she has, in her behavior toward me, informed me in a manner more elegant than had she told me a dozen times."

It was an effort to calm herself, but Elizabeth did so ruthlessly, for rancor would not serve her. There was little reason to be angry, for the situation was resolved, though the manner of that resolution was still unknown to her. Jane would not wish Elizabeth to vent her anger on this man, and given his behavior of late, Elizabeth knew it would be better to release the wrongs of the past. But there were a few matters she wished to clarify, even if this conversation had gone far afield of her original intention.

"I apologize, Mr. Darcy, for I do not wish to accuse—rather, I want to understand. Then you all persuaded Mr. Bingley to depart from Netherfield using those arguments?"

"Not exactly," said Mr. Darcy. "Bingley departed for town the day after the ball, a matter of business calling him there. His sisters and I did not follow until two days later."

Elizabeth regarded him, wondering if there was something of which he was not speaking. The gentleman appeared to feel her scrutiny, for he clarified:

"The primary argument in favor of staying in London came from his sisters, for I saw no reason to argue against your sister. I provided my opinion of Miss Bennet's indifference—for which I have already apologized—but had little else to contribute."

The girls interrupted their conversation then, Miss Darcy appealing to her brother for a purchase, while the girls did the same to their elder sisters. Elizabeth regarded them with exasperation, not only for the interruption but also because they were begging their sisters for their purchases when they had already used their allowance. There was little enough to be done, so Elizabeth shared a look with Mary and agreed to make a small purchase for them.

With glee, the three girls took their items and exited the haberdashers, eagerly looking about for the next shop to patronize. Elizabeth looked to Lydia, noting her looks were sly as if she were planning some great mischief. With a nod at Mr. Darcy, Elizabeth took herself to her sister's side, fixing her with a stern expression, one Lydia had routinely ignored in the past.

"Do not suppose we will pay for an excess of unneeded items, Lydia." When Lydia might have protested, Elizabeth shook her head. "The purpose of today's outing was not to dispense with as much of our funds as possible. It was to enjoy the company of your new friend and come to know her better."

Lydia, it seemed, understood Elizabeth was determined not to be moved. While she showed her displeasure with a huff, she nodded and joined the other girls, and they began walking toward the millinery. Elizabeth turned and noted that Mr. Darcy was nearby, his expression informing Elizabeth he had heard her admonishment. The gentleman's smile seemed to indicate his opinion of her sisters had not worsened by what he had overheard.

"It is the way of younger siblings, is it not? There is always something new, something tempting, and rarely does the thought of restraint pass their minds."

Elizabeth regarded him with interest. "Do you suggest your sister is also afflicted with the same?"

"I think there are few who are not," replied Mr. Darcy. "You may suppose it is silly for me, a wealthy man, to counsel my sister to restraint or frugality, but it is what my father taught me, a quality I have never found reason to question."

"On the contrary, Mr. Darcy," said Elizabeth, "it is laudable to think that way when you can afford whatever you wish to purchase."

Mr. Darcy's lips twitched, and his eyes danced with merriment. "That is not precisely true, Miss Elizabeth. For example, I doubt very much that I could afford to purchase Chatsworth."

Elizabeth returned his grin. "I was speaking of possibilities, Mr. Darcy."

The gentleman easily agreed with her. "My father never agreed with the notion that a child should receive everything for which she asks, even if the means exist to make the purchase of no consequence."

"Perhaps you should speak to my sisters," said Elizabeth. "They can rarely be bothered to listen to us. They might listen to you more."

The gentleman agreed, and they left the shop after their sisters. Seeing that Mary was following the girls, her watchful eyes fixed on them, Elizabeth suggested they visit the bookseller, a suggestion to which Mr. Darcy was all too ready to agree.

Mr. Lodge's shop was a tiny nook, settled between the general store and another equally large merchant. The man himself was thin and tall, tufts of greying hair all that remained on his head, defying gravity and giving him the look of a scarecrow. He was a pleasant man, one Elizabeth had known since she was old enough to read; since he had learned of Elizabeth's love of the written word, he had often allowed her to sit in the confines of his little shop and read, eager to hear her opinions of the works she browsed.

"Miss Elizabeth," said he as he saw her enter. "I see you have brought a gentleman with you today. I hope he is as eager as you to peruse my selection."

An upturned eyebrow on Mr. Darcy proved to be all the gentleman needed, for he smiled and nodded. "Should you see my library at my estate, you would know that I too am a lover of the written word."

"Excellent," said the shopkeeper with a smile. "Then please, look to your heart's content."

The man returned to a book of ledgers he had been studying, and Elizabeth and Darcy went deeper into the small shop. While there, they debated the merits of everything from histories to poetry, each sharing their tastes and defending their preferences. That last, Elizabeth found to be surprisingly unnecessary, for their preferences were aligned more than Elizabeth might have expected. Mr. Darcy proved himself well-read, for more than once he found a work she had not read and recommended it to her, and once, to her father. An erudite man, she decided. Yet, there was still the question of how Mr. Bingley had made his way back to Jane, though by now Elizabeth was certain she already had the answer.

At length, when they made their way from the shop, Elizabeth turned to him and said: "It appears you have followed your own advice concerning the efficacy of extensive reading."

Mr. Darcy appeared to understand her reference at once. "If you recall, I suggested the need for reading pertained to a *woman's* accomplishments?"

"I recall it well," replied Elizabeth. "But if I may be so bold, I suggest it is also desirable in a man, for I have often met men who believe they are learned, yet their lack of knowledge of literature and the world around them render their claims suspect at best."

"Yes," replied Mr. Darcy. "I have met a few of those myself, including your cousin if you will allow me to drop a name."

The gentleman's words could not but provoke Elizabeth's amusement, for she had been thinking of the very man when she spoke. Agree though she did, however, Elizabeth still had one question to ask, and she did not mean to be denied.

"If I may impose upon you one more time," said she, fixing the gentleman with a serious look belying her previous amusement, "there is another matter about which I would ask. I understand your account of what motivated you in the matter of Mr. Bingley, but I still cannot account for his sudden return to my sister. Can you not explain?"

Darcy had expected this last question. It was fortunate he had already navigated the worst of the shoals that might sink his ship long before it reached its destination, that of a successful proposal. Success was by no means guaranteed, but the conversation they had exchanged had taught him that all was not yet lost. It was with this in mind that he bent his thoughts to responding to her question.

"You must suspect by now that I had a hand in his return."

"I do," confirmed she. "Nothing else makes much sense at this late date, and Jane informed me of it herself. Yet I do not know why you did it, for everything that motivated you was still in force when Mr. Bingley visited my sister in London. If that was so, then how did you come to encourage him to return?"

"The fallacy in your thinking is the notion that those motivations were still in force."

Miss Elizabeth regarded him curiously. "Then how did they change?"

"Do you remember meeting my cousin Fitzwilliam in the woods of Rosings the day we departed from Kent?"

"He informed you of our conversation!" exclaimed she.

"Not at once," replied Darcy. He paused and gave her a shamefaced look. "Fitzwilliam made more of my account than I intended, for I never mentioned it to suggest boasting. Regardless, when we discussed the matter and I learned how upset you became, it was easy to deduce I was in error."

"How could you have known? I might have been angry for no other reason than the loss of a prospective mark for my sister."

"That was a possible interpretation, yes," agreed Darcy. "But only if one did not *know* you, Miss Elizabeth."

"How so?" asked she with a frown.

"Your cousin's actions the night of the ball were not obscure. I could see that he wished to have you for a wife by the time the first dance ended."

Miss Elizabeth gaped at him. "But you watched with amusement! It was my firm opinion that you and Miss Bingley considered Mr. Collins nothing more than my due."

"What Miss Bingley thought I cannot say, for she has vouchsafed no opinion on the subject. For my part, my initial entertainment was for the parson's ineptitude. It was not long before I became disgusted with him, in part because of your discomfort, and also because he did not attempt to improve himself. It was obvious he was not aware he was causing you any distress.

"When I arrived in Kent, I expected to be introduced to you as the wife of the parson—it was a welcome surprise to learn you had not married the man. Thus, when I learned of your distress upon learning of my interference in the matter of your sister, it was easy to connect that with what I suspected was your refusal of Mr. Collins. If *you* refused a proposal because you did not favor the suitor, I judged *Miss Bennet* to be of the same moral fiber. When I had that information, I reflected on my impression of Miss Bennet's response to my friend and learned to my regret that my understanding of the situation was faulty. And that led to my confession to my friend, for my new understanding of Miss Bennet's unwillingness to accept a proposal if she did not favor it rendered my argument that she might accept because of her mother's insistence unsound."

Miss Elizabeth watched him as he explained, giving little hint of her response to his explanation. For all Darcy knew, she might consider his account the grossest of falsehoods. Darcy was prepared to argue its truth, though he would not consider explaining those points he had not chosen to reveal. Now was not the time to explain his need to propose, and the points he had left out would betray them to her.

"There are many leaps of logic in your explanation," said Miss Bennet at length. "So much that I am uncertain I can follow them or fathom how you reached them."

"And yet they all made sense to me at the time," replied Darcy easily. "Events have proven my epiphany true and my initial judgment false. I am glad I made amends when I did, for neither your sister nor my friend deserved to be separated under such circumstances when their affection was true."

"Miss Bingley does not think the same way."

"If you will pardon me, I care little for Miss Bingley's opinion. Miss Bingley weighs everything by wealth and promotion in society. I am afraid I do not, and, more importantly, her brother does not. I would much rather concern myself with my friend's happiness than Miss Bingley's desire to rise in others' estimation."

"Then it is fortunate you are the man you are," said Miss Elizabeth, giving him a nod, accompanied by a soft smile. "Many would consider Mr. Bingley's background a detriment, even if they appreciated the man. I thank you for your actions, sir, for I have your integrity to thank for my sister's current happiness."

At that moment, the two youngest Bennets, with Georgiana, approached them, calling greetings, chattering about what they had done and seen. Miss Mary and his cousin were following them, apparently easy in each other's company, for they walked close behind, conversation flowing between them with easiness. Then Bingley and Miss Bennet approached from wherever they had gone, completing their group. Again, Darcy was treated to the sight of Miss Bennet's happiness, which was clear in the glow that seemed to surround her like a halo. Even in Bingley, there was a subtle difference from his usual cheer, for while he had always been a joyous sort of man, now he appeared more confident as if Miss Bennet completed him.

The company soon turned toward Longbourn, their composition much as it had been when they had come to Meryton. Darcy basked in Miss Elizabeth's company, though they exchanged little of any consequence, a welcome relief after the fraught moments of their previous tête-à-tête. In this easy manner, they passed half the distance to Longbourn.

Then Darcy became aware of a subject of which the youngest girls were speaking, unsurprising given what Darcy knew of their preferences. Darcy might have predicted in advance they would draw Georgiana into their excitement, though he had rarely seen his sister so enthusiastic about anything before.

"There is an assembly in two days," said Miss Lydia. It appeared they had been speaking of dancing, though Darcy had heard little of what they had been saying. "Have you attended a dance recently, Georgiana?"

"I have never attended," said Georgiana, a hint of surprise about her.

"Never attended!" exclaimed Miss Kitty as if she could not comprehend such a calamity.

"Surely you know how to dance," said Miss Lydia.

"I do," replied Georgiana. "Brother has engaged an instructor, and I have danced with him and with my cousins to practice."

"But you have never attended?" demanded Miss Lydia, apparently scandalized.

"I am not yet out."

"That is strange," said Miss Lydia. "I am a year younger than you, and I have been out since last summer."

"That is not entirely accurate, Lydia," interjected Miss Elizabeth.

The girl looked at her crossly, but Miss Elizabeth was undeterred.

"Papa agreed to allow you to attend local functions because Kitty came out. But as you are not yet sixteen, you are *not* out. If we attended any social events outside this community, Papa would not allow you to attend."

"Oh, I could persuade Papa," said Miss Lydia with unconcern.

Darcy's observation had been that Mr. Bennet's parenting style was more than a little lackadaisical, meaning his capitulation was a distinct possibility. Miss Elizabeth's pursed lips informed him that she both did not agree and she understood her sister might be correct. Sensing a disagreement might be in the offing, Darcy felt obliged to interject his opinion.

"You must understand the society we inhabit, Miss Lydia. In London, a young woman does not come out until she has both reached the age of eighteen and had her presentation to the queen. Georgiana will not come out for another two years."

"But Brother," said Georgiana with more beseeching than he might have expected, "surely, I might be permitted the same freedom as Lydia. Should I not have some small taste of what to expect before I enter London society?"

Fitzwilliam chortled, saying: "Our little Georgiana appears to have gained much in a brief acquaintance with the youngest Bennets. Two weeks ago, I doubt she would have made such an application."

Georgiana showed her maturity by sticking her tongue out at her cousin; Fitzwilliam's response of a funny face showed *his*. Then Georgiana turned back to Darcy, her pleading a quality he had rarely seen from her before.

"You wish to attend the assembly, Georgiana?" clarified he, wondering if he still knew his sister as the shy creature she had been the previous week.

"With your permission, of course," said Georgiana.

"Oh, that would be lovely!" exclaimed Miss Kitty. "We could introduce her to all the officers; she would not want for a dance partner all night!"

That was not a ringing endorsement in Darcy's opinion, and even Georgiana did not appear to agree with the suggestion. Again, Fitzwilliam interposed his opinion.

"While I would not counsel throwing caution to the wind, I cannot but suppose an assembly in a small neighborhood like this would be a good place for our Georgiana to obtain her first taste of society. As an unknown quantity in Meryton, there would be little pressure on her."

Darcy acknowledged his cousin made an excellent point, but he was also hesitant about it. This was his sister, the last member of his family, and the most precious person in the world to him. Idly, Darcy wondered if this was what all men felt when their daughters approached maturity. Perhaps if he was fortunate, he and Miss Elizabeth would only produce sons, for he could not imagine this with *his* daughter.

"I think it is an excellent notion," said Miss Elizabeth, her look suggesting she thought he might forbid her. "My sisters and I will keep Miss Darcy company, and we shall take care of her sensibilities."

With such a promise, how could Darcy possibly think to refuse? As such, he made the only decision he could.

"Then I suppose you shall get your first taste of society in two days, Georgiana."

Before he could say another word, his sister flew into his arms, thanking him and exclaiming her excitement. Then before he could understand what was happening, she had returned to the youngest Bennets and was chattering excitedly with them. The sight was enough to melt Darcy's heart; he had made the right choice.

"Shall we tell her that she will dance only with close acquaintances?" asked Fitzwilliam, laughter in his tone.

"I suggest you allow her to bask in her excitement for the moment," replied Miss Elizabeth with a grin. "Telling her when she has calmed will be soon enough."

Fitzwilliam laughed. "Yes, I suppose you are correct, Miss Elizabeth."

He walked away with Miss Mary, and the company moved down the path again. Miss Elizabeth fell in by Darcy's side.

"That was well done, Mr. Darcy. It would have disappointed her if you had refused. She will not come to any harm in our company; this I pledge to you."

"Thank you, Miss Elizabeth."

Darcy did not mention how her opinion had tipped the scales for him, but he did not forget it. Soon, he would make clear to her just how much he respected her opinion.

CHAPTER IX

"*Y*our scowl is so fearsome that your letter *must* be from Lady Catherine."

Darcy turned that scowl on Fitzwilliam, who approached him from the door to the library. In his hand, the offending missive — which was, indeed, from his detestable aunt — burned his fingers as if it were aflame. Darcy's first inclination had been to hurl it into the fire and make its immolation a reality, but he had not regained the power of movement after having read her repulsive words.

"It is," said Darcy, his response clipped. "I have half a mind to go to Kent directly and take her over my knee, for it is clear she deserves every hint of the corporal punishment I can mete out on her foolishness."

"More of her threats?"

Unwilling to read it again, Darcy thrust the pages at his cousin. "You had best look for yourself, for it will provoke me to violence if I read it again."

Fitzwilliam regarded Darcy as he accepted the letter. "Perhaps we should discuss this concept of corporal punishment you raised. The notion of my aunt stretched across your knee while you administer a spanking has great potential."

It did to Darcy too, but he contented himself with a grunt, pacing the floor in his rage while Fitzwilliam scanned their aunt's latest folly. If Darcy was honest with himself, the matter had now become one of pride, for he was not about to allow Lady Catherine to browbeat him into anything. It was imperative he defeat her intrigues, for he would not allow so odious a woman as she any victory.

"She threatens to make Georgiana's misstep known at once if you do not bow to her will," observed Fitzwilliam.

"And tells me this is my last warning," snarled Darcy. "What a woman she is! How can we possibly be related to such a hard, unfeeling, selfish virago as she?"

"That is little less than my father has said all these years," replied Fitzwilliam.

His cousin seated himself on a chair and watched Darcy for several moments. "Sit, Darcy," growled he at length. "Your pacing is making me dizzy."

Darcy did as he was asked, though he directed a glare at his cousin, one Fitzwilliam did not even seem to notice.

"What do you mean to do about this?"

With a helpless shrug, Darcy said: "There is little enough I *can* do. I must propose to Miss Elizabeth and soon, and we must marry soon after."

"Let us dispense with this bit of the farcical, Darcy," replied Fitzwilliam. "You are not unaware of Lady Catherine's peculiar brand of dogged determination. Even if you should marry, you must know that will not deter her; she will do as she threatens out of spite."

Darcy grimaced, for he knew his cousin was correct after a fashion. "Then I suppose we must draw this out for as long as possible, for your father is the only member of the family with any hope of stopping her."

Fitzwilliam gave him a level look. "Then what is this all about? If you have known all along that Lady Catherine would not relent, why have you pursued this course with such dogged determination?"

"Because I want to have Miss Elizabeth for a wife, I suppose," said Darcy, confirming his cousin's earlier charge. "I still believe removing all possibility of marriage with Anne may prompt Lady Catherine to desist. She will snarl and snap and will abuse both myself and Miss Elizabeth, but she will not wish to provoke gossip when there is no more purpose to be served."

"Then there is little time for delay," replied Fitzwilliam. "Tonight is the assembly, and possibly your last chance to recommend yourself to Miss Elizabeth. You will need to act within the next day or two, for with this bit of insanity," Fitzwilliam shook the letter still in his hand, "I doubt Lady Catherine will wait another week."

As if on cue, Georgiana entered the room, her face stormy with displeasure. On her heels, Miss Bingley entered the room, with her brother close behind. No two siblings could have looked less alike than the Bingleys at that moment, for Miss Bingley's countenance was discontented as had been her wont of late, while Bingley's was diverted, nearly laughing. Then the look he threw at his sister was exasperated, even as his glance at Georgiana was full of empathy.

"Brother!" said Georgiana, a hint of wildness in her voice.

"Georgiana," replied Darcy, rising to greet her, accepting her into his arms. "How has your morning been?"

"Long and trying," whispered Georgiana. She pushed away and did not quite look at Miss Bingley, though Darcy was certain her reply had concerned the other woman, and in a normal voice said: "I am so anticipating this evening, that I can hardly stand the wait! What fun we shall have, and I shall enjoy it all with Kitty and Lydia and Elizabeth too!"

"It is nothing more than a country dance," sneered Miss Bingley before Darcy could answer. "And a poor one at that, if the last assembly we attended was any indication."

The look Georgiana gave him told Darcy all he needed to know of her feelings, even had he not known of Miss Bingley's behavior the past two days since they had told her of their intention to attend the assembly. Darcy gave Georgiana the barest hint of a nod, informing her of his support, not that she should be in doubt of it. Georgiana stood a little straighter at the sight of it as if she now had a wall to her back and could turn to face her attacker.

"It is but my first time attending," said Georgiana in response to Miss Bingley's meanness. "I know it will not equal events in London, and yet it will be special *because* it is my first time."

"Georgiana, dearest," said Miss Bingley, her tone sickeningly sweet, "it is a mark of your unfortunate inexperience, but the Bennet sisters are not ladies with whom you should associate. This assembly would no more prepare you for society than an afternoon of walking around a paddock would prepare you to ride a horse. It would be best if you avoided the so-called *festivities* this evening and kept your innocence and anticipation intact."

Georgiana gaped at Miss Bingley; Darcy found he could do no less. Did the woman not understand how patronizing her comment was? At the same time, Fitzwilliam snorted, though a glance in his direction informed Darcy he was diverted by Miss Bingley's conceit rather than affronted at her temerity. While he might have expected Fitzwilliam to speak at once to prick her arrogance, instead he leaned back in his chair and regarded her with an expression bespeaking equal parts anticipation for her set down and disdain for her person.

"Kitty and Lydia are my friends, Miss Bingley," said Georgiana. Her even tone should have told Miss Bingley that she was treading on dangerous ground, not that Darcy expected the woman would recognize it.

"Friendship between those of such disparate backgrounds is impractical, Georgiana," cooed Miss Bingley, proving Darcy's conjecture. "Knowledge of how to uphold your nobility will not come from associating with those who are so wholly unsuitable. You would be better served to refrain."

"I am interested to hear your definition of 'disparate backgrounds,' Miss Bingley," interjected Fitzwilliam. "I must wonder what you mean. Are the Bennet sisters not the daughters of a gentleman? Is Georgiana not the same?"

The woman shot him a glare, but Fitzwilliam regarded her calmly, a hint of a sardonic grin stretched across his face. She understood his inference as well as if he had come out and told her without disguise that her situation did not compare to their position in society. But she refrained from responding other than to give him a superior sniff.

"Miss Bingley," said Georgiana, her stand implying she had endured as much as she could, "there is nothing the matter with my new friends. If my brother considered them unsuitable, he would not have introduced me to their acquaintance."

Miss Bingley, it seemed, had not expected Georgiana to deny her so readily, though how she could have missed Georgiana's growing annoyance these past days, Darcy could not say. The look she turned on Darcy was beseeching, more hope than conviction, but that did not prevent her from making her case.

"Why you introduced them to her, I cannot say, Mr. Darcy. But I must remind you of your opinion of the Bennets after we came to Hertfordshire. If you and my brother must keep up appearances, I understand and agree. But I shall stay home with your sister and keep her company. You have my solemn promise to ensure she remains unblemished from the influence of the uncouth locals."

"My sister is correct, Miss Bingley," said Darcy, unwilling to allow her continued insolence. "If I did not consider the Bennets appropriate acquaintances, I would not have introduced her."

The woman gaped as if she did not know him. Behind her, Bingley watched, his expression tight with displeasure.

"Then you mean to allow her to attend?"

"Was it not I who gave her permission?"

If anything, Miss Bingley's look hardened. "Then it shall be as you say. Do not concern yourself, Mr. Darcy, for I pledge I shall keep your sister safe from those who would damage her sensibilities."

By that, Darcy was certain she meant to keep Georgiana's company to herself and away from anyone in the neighborhood. Georgiana noted the same if her huff of annoyance was any hint of her feelings.

"That will be quite unnecessary, Miss Bingley. I highly doubt any manner of poor behavior would affect my sister in one evening. She will be with the Miss Bennets, who have spoken of their desire for her continued society and their eagerness to associate with her at tonight's entertainment. I have no doubt she will be adequately protected."

"I shall," said Georgiana. "My friends will be with me, and they have promised to stand up with me since my partners will be limited."

It took no great powers of discernment to understand that Miss Bingley did not appreciate his failure to agree with her. Georgiana turned to Darcy, a twinkle in her eye. "Do you intend to dance tonight, Brother?"

"Yes," replied Darcy. "I must uphold the honor of the family, after all."

Miss Bingley huffed her dissatisfaction. But Georgiana ignored her.

"Then what shall we do about the first dance?"

"I shall claim your first dance if you will," interjected Fitzwilliam. He shot Darcy a smirk and added: "I suspect Darcy wishes to ask a certain special lady for the first dance."

The look of displeasure on Miss Bingley's face became positively forbidding.

"If you are amenable, Georgiana," said Darcy.

"Of course!" said the girl. "I look forward to it."

They remained together for some time after, for Georgiana appeared unwilling to allow Miss Bingley to corner her for more of her brand of persuasion, and Miss Bingley was intent upon protecting her interests in them both when she was not brooding about what she suspected would occur that evening. At length, as the afternoon lengthened, Miss Bingley finally excused herself—by this time, she was in high dudgeon—to prepare for their repast before their departure and her wardrobe for the evening. Those left behind exchanged exasperated glances.

"I apologize, Darcy, Miss Darcy," said Bingley when the echoes of her footsteps faded down the hall. "She has become nigh unendurable; I have half a mind to send her to the north."

"She means to ruin my fun tonight," said Georgiana, a hint of a plaintive whine entering her voice.

"Do not concern yourself," said Bingley, the ever-present jollity returning to his tone. "We will ensure she does not importune you. Once you are in the company of the Bennets, I doubt she will have an opportunity to pull you away."

Darcy was uncertain his friend had the right of it, but he contented himself with smiling at his sister to inform her of his support. He could always take a direct hand against Miss Bingley if it proved necessary. From the way Fitzwilliam regarded her, he would relish the prospect of telling Miss Bingley exactly what he thought of her. The woman frustrated Darcy enough that he might just allow Fitzwilliam his head.

"Stand up straight, girls! Make the most of your figures, and your gentlemen will not hold their countenances when they come.

Elizabeth regarded her mother, feeling more than a hint of exasperation well up in her breast. Mrs. Bennet had been chivvying them since their arrival, putting them in the best position where Mr. Bingley and Mr. Darcy would see them the moment they entered the room. She also had Mary, Kitty, and Lydia lined up beside them, no doubt hoping Colonel Fitzwilliam would take a fancy to one of them. That the colonel had yet given no indication of interest in any of her daughters, and if he *had*, it was undoubtedly Mary, and not Lydia, her favorite, did not discourage her.

Furthermore, this business of interpreting Mr. Darcy's interest in Elizabeth herself was a source of frustration, for all Elizabeth was coming to the conclusion that her mother may be correct. Elizabeth was of two minds about it, uncertain as she was whether Mr. Darcy was a compatible partner. She was certain she and Mr. Darcy would find their way to each other with far greater ease should Mrs. Bennet simply remove herself from the equation, but her mother would not see that. In Mrs. Bennet's mind, not only was the prize far more important than any quaint notions like love, respect, and compatibility, but any triumph must necessarily involve her. Otherwise, Elizabeth might refuse Mr. Darcy out of hand, and they simply could not have *that*.

As if to validate Elizabeth's thoughts, Mrs. Bennet sidled up to her. "Now, Lizzy, do not rattle on as you usually do. Mr. Darcy has been so agreeable of late that I dare say our impression of him in the autumn was quite inaccurate. And he has paid exclusive attention to *you*, though I thought to direct him at Lydia when he returned."

The notion was laughable; a shallow, ignorant girl of Lydia's ilk would never attract a worldly man such as Mr. Darcy. But Elizabeth knew better than to cast shade on her mother's favorite and declined to reply. Mrs. Bennet, it seemed, did not appreciate how she demurred.

"Elizabeth, Mr. Darcy has given every reason to expect a proposal. I trust you will not reject and abuse him as you did Mr. Collins?"

"I shall act," replied Elizabeth, "in a manner which will constitute my happiness." Seeing the storm clouds rolling in on Mrs. Bennet's brow and not wishing to provoke an argument, she added: "Mr. Darcy *has* been remarkably civil, Mama. He is not like Mr. Collins."

This satisfied Mrs. Bennet, though Elizabeth had said very little. "Excellent. Now, present yourself to your best advantage, Lizzy, and you will provoke him to propose before you might have expected."

It should not surprise the discerning reader that Elizabeth was feeling cross by the time the Netherfield party made their appearance, and one facet of that appearance did not improve her mood. Miss Bingley paused in the door as if for effect, her behavior reminiscent of the first time Elizabeth had ever seen the Bingley party the previous year. It was, of course, much less effective than it had been then, for the Bingleys were now known in Meryton, and they had arrived before the assembly began. Elizabeth attributed that to Mr. Bingley's desire to arrive on time, for she knew Miss Bingley would not have come at all if she had her way.

The rest of the party, however, did not await her posturing. They moved to the Bennets at once, the gentlemen grinning their welcome, while Georgiana skipped ahead of them, eager to join her new friends.

"How happy I am to see you!" exclaimed she when she had greeted them all. "What fun we shall have."

Kitty and Lydia crowded around her, and the girls moved a little distance away, whispering and giggling among themselves. Miss Bingley, Elizabeth noted, did not appear pleased, but Mr. Bingley grasped her arm and directed her to Jane, preventing her from following them. Colonel Fitzwilliam watched the girls with affection, even if he kept a wary eye on his charge. Elizabeth's attention, however, was soon captured by Mr. Darcy, for he approached her directly and bowed.

"Miss Elizabeth," said he. "You are a vision tonight."

Unaccountably bashful, Elizabeth dropped her gaze to the floor, glancing up at him from behind her eyelashes. "Thank you, Mr. Darcy. I hope you have come prepared to dance."

The gentleman gave her such a grin as she had never seen from him before. "As you know, dancing is not my favorite activity. But I hope to acquit myself well. To that end, if I may be so bold, might I request your first sets?"

The gasp from Miss Bingley—and the way she regarded him as if he had betrayed her—informed Elizabeth that she was not the only one surprised by his request. When they had danced at Netherfield, Elizabeth had been unable to understand why he had asked her at all, so determined had he seemed to be displeased, his purpose apparently to find fault rather than attempt to enjoy himself in a situation in which such gratification was impossible.

"But your sister, sir," said Elizabeth, gathering herself for a response. "It is her first Assembly! Should you not dance the first with her?"

"Your conjecture might be correct had she and Fitzwilliam not already agreed between themselves to partner for the first dance." Mr. Darcy nodded to his cousin, who was standing near Georgiana and Elizabeth's two youngest sisters, in conversation with Mary. "Thus, I am available for those sets and will dance the second with my sister. I should like to dance the first with a special lady."

Before Elizabeth could muster a response, Miss Bingley's patience snapped, and she could not refrain from speaking. "Oh, Mr. Darcy, how diverting you are!" Miss Bingley's poisonous look at Elizabeth belied her expressed amusement. "I am certain your sister was not speaking of *Miss Eliza* when she suggested you secure a special partner."

"Regardless of what my sister inferred," said Mr. Darcy, all but ignoring the woman though he was nominally responding to her, "the choice is mine, and I wish to ask Miss Elizabeth. If you are agreeable?"

There was nothing to do but respond, though Elizabeth's suspicions were becoming unendurable. "Of course, Mr. Darcy. I shall be happy to cede those sets to you."

Miss Bingley stamped her foot in annoyance, but Elizabeth could spare no attention for the unpleasant woman. Instead, her every thought was focused on Mr. Darcy and, perhaps equally important, how she could induce him to share what he was thinking with her. Something was happening in all this that she could not quite grasp but spoke to something beyond a man's interest in her. Elizabeth meant to have that answer.

While they waited for the dancing to begin, Elizabeth stood beside Mr. Darcy and a silent and displeased Miss Bingley. There was little enough they could say to each another, for Miss Bingley did not appear in a mood to allow them to converse to any great extent. Of course, when the music started and Mr. Darcy extended his hand to take hers, Miss Bingley's ability to interfere ended.

"Mr. Darcy," said Elizabeth the moment an opportunity presented itself, "there is something strange happening here, and I wish to know what it is."

The man appeared as wary as a newborn colt. "To what do you refer?"

"Your appearance here in Hertfordshire, your actions, your insistence in putting yourself in my company, not the least of which is your surprising request for my first sets when you do not enjoy dancing."

"That is not entirely accurate," said the gentleman. "I can enjoy dancing well enough with the right partner."

Elizabeth fixed narrowed eyes on him, unimpressed with his deflection. "So now you consider me 'handsome enough to tempt you?'"

That he did not recognize her turn of phrase could not be hidden. "You are more than handsome enough, Miss Elizabeth. I consider you one of the prettiest women of my acquaintance."

"You do," echoed Elizabeth. "By my reckoning, you did not always think so."

"And yet I do now," replied he. Elizabeth heard an earnestness in his voice that she did not think he could feign. "I will own that you did not captivate me immediately, but it did not take long before you held me in your thrall."

Elizabeth shook off his flattery, for she did not wish to allow him to move her from her purpose. "Will you not explain this to me? Our interactions in Kent were not changed to any significant degree, but when I returned home, and you are making love to my family and showering me with your attention. If you have some purpose in mind, I should like to know what it is."

He seemed pained by her comment, but he gamely replied. "I have no objection to explaining myself, Miss Elizabeth. But I should not like to do so in this setting where anyone might overhear."

Elizabeth regarded him for a long moment. "Then will you meet with me on the estate tomorrow? I walk out most mornings. We would have the privacy you require."

"If you share the location, I will come," agreed Mr. Darcy.

They spoke intently, Elizabeth informing him of where they could meet, and explaining how he could reach it. When that was complete, they turned their attention back to the dance. It could not be supposed that two people who had just shared such an exchange could return to their previous easiness, and in this case, that was unfortunately true. Their interactions were halting, yet Elizabeth felt herself safe with the man, strange since she had just demanded to know what he was about.

When the dance ended and they parted, Elizabeth was pleased to note that his civility endured, for after dancing with his sister, he danced with Jane and then Mary, and even seemed to enjoy himself with Lydia and Kitty. There were a few other ladies with whom she stood up, but that was the extent of his civility, for after a time he took position by the side of the floor, watching the dancers. Much to Miss Bingley's disgust, he did not solicit her hand. The forbidding glare with which he observed the previous assembly was, mercifully, absent.

For Elizabeth's part, she danced with local men, with Mr. Bingley, with Colonel Fitzwilliam, and even with Georgiana a time or two. They were all pleasant, but Elizabeth could not focus on them, for her mind was filled with the important meeting on the morrow.

"You appear distracted," said Colonel Fitzwilliam during their time together.

Elizabeth realized belatedly she had said little to him. Far from being offended, the man watched her, concern for her unmistakable.

"Unless I am mistaken, I know the reason for it," said he before she could respond. "I cannot but imagine you are confused, Miss Elizabeth, and I will not attempt to alleviate it, for I know that is Darcy's task. I would only ask you for one favor."

"What would that be?" asked Elizabeth, curious.

"Give Darcy a chance and do not judge until he has told you all."

"Then you know what this is all about?"

"Some of it," acknowledged the colonel. "But the rest I cannot know, for it exists in Darcy's heart. Remember, when he speaks to you, that my cousin is not always adept at sharing his feelings. If you remember nothing else, that thought will sustain you. Whatever he says to you, you may consider his true feelings to be tenfold more powerful than what he can relate, and you will not go amiss."

Elizabeth regarded him and nodded. "I shall keep an open mind."

Later, when the Bennets returned to their home and Elizabeth to her room, she reflected on the colonel's advice. It was perhaps the most apropos she had ever received. Elizabeth determined to do exactly as he said.

CHAPTER X

"Mr. Darcy! I had not expected to see you here this early!"
The gentleman, who had been pacing the path in the moments before Elizabeth arrived turned to look at her, an expression of welcome and something she could not define in his smile and his eyes. "I found I could not sleep, so I came early."

"Is what you wish to say to me that difficult?"

Mr. Darcy's smile turned a little rueful. "In some respects, it is, for it will betray matters I should prefer to keep secret. Yet, I know I must inform you of all, for we can settle nothing between us until you have my full account."

Elizabeth regarded him, wondering at the ominous implications of his statement. She had departed Longbourn that morning, more than an hour before she had arranged to meet him on that path near the border between Longbourn and Netherfield. Arriving early, she had told herself, would give her time to think about the situation. The reality was she could determine little other than what she already knew, as a largely sleepless night had already informed her.

But it had always been thus for Elizabeth. While she might have learned nothing from additional consideration, it would calm her, render her better able to hear him and judge his words, to understand

and respond. But he had anticipated her, the time to think she needed now unavailable.

Elizabeth could not blame the gentleman. He was in such a state of perturbation, that it suddenly became clear that his communication would be perilous, far more momentous than she had expected. And she had expected much. There was nothing to do but invite him to make his communication.

"Well, Mr. Darcy," said Elizabeth aloud as all of this was passing through her mind, "I suppose we must proceed with your tale. If you do not mind, I should like to do so in a more comfortable setting. There is a bench a little further down this path—shall we not proceed there?"

Mr. Darcy cocked his head to the side, even as he extended his arm to her. "I recall passing it, though I was not cognizant enough of my surroundings to take any true notice. It is an odd place for a bench, is it not?"

As she accepted his arm, Elizabeth nodded. "Papa had it placed there some years ago. This is among my favorite paths, and as it is long, Papa decided I needed someplace to rest should I become fatigued."

"And do you?" asked the gentleman.

With a laugh, Elizabeth nodded. "Occasionally, I sit there for a time, but it is more because I do not wish my father's considerate gesture to go to waste than from any need."

As Mr. Darcy laughed, Elizabeth exclaimed: "But do not tell him!" Then she paused and added: "He suspects that is the reason I use it, but we maintain the fiction between us that I occasionally become fatigued."

The gentleman laughed, and they arrived at the bench. It was little more than a log laid by the side of the track, the top leveled and smoothed, the wood lacquered so it could better withstand the ravages of nature. It was not by any means a comfortable bench on which one could sit for hours, but it was situated in a lovely strand of trees, the glossy surface sparkling in dappled brilliance through the surrounding foliage, so recently sprung to life in that glorious spring.

Mr. Darcy guided her to the bench and saw her seated and comfortable, and when he saw she was, he began to pace. When he turned and passed by her again, she could see his eyebrows drawn down into a tight v, his agitation such as she had never seen before. Not for the first time, she wondered what might have caused such a composed gentleman to behave with such distress.

"Miss Elizabeth," said Darcy, trying to calm his troubled thoughts, "there is much I need to make clear to you. So much that I am uncertain what to say."

"I have always found," replied she with a smile, "the beginning is an excellent place to start."

"Ah, but sometimes it is difficult to pinpoint the beginning."

Miss Elizabeth smiled and nodded, and the precious nature of the woman before him struck Darcy with the force of a blacksmith's hammer. Many women would not have contradicted him or called him to account for himself, and many of his set would have preferred a quiet, compliant woman who would never dare question him. Darcy was not that sort. Did a man seek to cover the sun, to prevent its light from illuminating the world about him, bringing warmth in its wake? It was equally inconceivable that any man who claimed to esteem her could consider stealing this woman's voice and rendering her docile, biddable.

And yet, he could not help the trepidation that settled over his heart, for he could still lose all with his confession. If she took umbrage at his way of recommending himself or thought him capable of trying to force her hand to save himself from an unwanted marriage, he was uncertain what he could do to persuade her. But she needed the truth, so he forced himself to sit by her side and explain himself.

"The beginning, I suppose, must include an account of Wickham."

Miss Elizabeth's brows drew together. "Mr. Wickham? Does he have a part to play in whatever ails you?"

"He does," confirmed Darcy. "A part much larger than I might wish, such that I wish now in hindsight that I had taken action against him long ago. For you to understand what I must tell you, it is imperative for you to comprehend my past with him.

"As he no doubt told you, he is the son of my father's steward. Because of a dearth of young men my age on the estate, Wickham and I were companions from the time we were boys. But while I was his firmest friend, as we grew older, I came to understand his character was not what I might have wished."

"He caused trouble?" asked Miss Elizabeth.

Darcy sighed and put his hand on the bench beside his leg, leaning on it, recalling those days as the shadow of doubt concerning his friend settled over his heart. "At first, I did not recognize the signs. Then when I began to understand, I denied them. Surely my closest friend could not be so depraved. When I could no longer rationalize my observations, I went first to my father, and then to Fitzwilliam, my closest cousin."

The pain of those days washed over Darcy again, and he grasped his knees with his hands to avoid standing and pacing in front of her. Miss Elizabeth would not judge him if he showed his emotion, for she was an emotional woman. But if he did not keep his calm, he would never make it through his explanation.

"Mr. Wickham, as I recall, praised your father as the best of men."

Darcy would not help the rush of anger he felt at her comment. "Wickham used my father, Miss Elizabeth. While I cannot discount the possibility that he felt some affection, it was obvious in word and deed that Wickham considered my father an easy mark. And my father, a man so discerning in other matters, could see nothing of Wickham's character."

"Oh, Mr. Darcy," breathed Miss Elizabeth.

For the first time since sitting on the bench, Darcy looked up into her face. Not knowing how she felt about Wickham other than the testy words they had exchanged at Bingley's ball, he had not been certain if she would believe him. To his utter relief, the compassion on her face informed him that he had not needed to worry. Whatever affection she might have harbored toward Wickham was gone, forced out by the truth.

"You must not blame my father, Miss Elizabeth," said Darcy. "It is easier for one such as I, one who saw Wickham in unguarded moments, to understand his character than for my father, who only saw Wickham when he checked his baser nature. I have no wish to recount the many offenses on Wickham's part over the years, for they are not truly relevant to the subject. It is enough you understand Wickham has been my adversary for many years."

"I do understand, Mr. Darcy," said she.

Darcy nodded and continued to the worst part of his account. "Then he committed the worst betrayal, for he attempted to take my sister from me."

Elizabeth listened with horror to Mr. Darcy's account of Mr. Wickham's actions the previous summer, how he and a paramour had plotted to betray a young girl for her fortune. She shuddered to think of how they had almost succeeded and would have but for the most providential chance that led Mr. Darcy to discover their plan.

The foremost emotion in Elizabeth's breast was anger—anger for Mr. Wickham and the depravity necessary to target such a sweet girl as Georgiana for her dowry. There was a large amount of anger for herself for being so gullible as to believe his lies without a second thought as if she were a credulous girl, newly off leading strings. She should have been more discerning, more suspicious of his willingness to share what should have been a private matter with a new acquaintance. Mostly, however, her heart went out to Georgiana, for no one deserved to suffer as she had.

"Your poor sister, Mr. Darcy," said she, determined that she would do what she could to help the girl's bruised heart to heal. "What an abominable man Mr. Wickham was to have betrayed her in such a way."

Mr. Darcy regarded her. "Thank you for your belief, Miss Bennet. I expected I would need to show you some proof of my assertions before you would favor me with your trust.

"Did I not listen and believe Mr. Wickham without a second thought?" asked Elizabeth, not entirely rhetorically. "No, Mr. Darcy. Though I did not see the holes in Mr. Wickham's story before, what you have told me today has answered the questions I should have had when I listened to that cur."

"Thank you," said the gentleman, his sigh expressing his relief. "I will suggest that it is not in your nature to disbelieve another with so little consideration."

"That does not speak as well to my character as you would suggest," replied Elizabeth with no small measure of wryness. "I have always considered myself an excellent judge of character, and part of that is to assess the worthiness of those I meet.

"It is well, then, that you have acted, and he must now pay the price for his actions."

"Though it is late," replied Mr. Darcy with a nod, "I have taken steps to ensure he troubles no one again. He has another part to play in what I must relate, but he will never harm me or mine again."

Intrigued though Elizabeth was, she ignored that for the moment. "And your sister; she appears quite recovered from her ordeal."

Mr. Darcy's look at her brimmed with warmth. "The welcome she has received since she arrived in Hertfordshire has especially affected her. Your sisters have inspired her confidence, and I dare say you have played no small part in that yourself."

Welcome though his response was, Elizabeth could only nod before she turned back to other matters. "We all esteem her, Mr. Darcy. But what you have related has not explained your behavior in full. Might I assume you have more to relate?"

"I should not be surprised at your acuity, Miss Elizabeth. Yes, there is more to this tale, and while I hesitate to share it, I know I must."

"Can it be any worse than what you have already shared?"

Darcy grimaced. "In some ways, Wickham's behavior is but a drop in the water compared with what will come next, and he played some part in it."

"Then please tell me, sir."

While Mr. Darcy had given the impression of wishing to rise to pace several times during their tête-à-tête, he had steadfastly remained seated beside her, resisting his impulse. At that moment, however, he surged to his feet and paced beside the bench, his agitation increased tenfold from what it had been before. Elizabeth could hardly imagine what could be more difficult to relate than what he had already shared. And yet, it appeared he was more loath to speak than he had been before. At length, he ceased his pacing, and while he did not sit, he approached her, planted himself before her, his feet spread shoulder-width as if he was rooting himself against the gale about to blow against him.

"While you were at Rosings," said he, "I assume you heard something of my aunt's desire for an alliance between my cousin and me?"

"I heard about it before I ever entered Kent," said Elizabeth, feeling the shame for listening to Mr. Wickham enter her heart again. "Mr. Wickham mentioned it to me when he visited a few days before I left Longbourn for Kent."

This did not seem to disturb Mr. Darcy, for he nodded. "Yes, I can well imagine it, for Wickham often taunted me about my future married to a woman colorless and cross. In this, he does not know as much as he thinks, for Anne can be personable when she wants to be. But that is a subject about which I do not wish to speak in any detail. As you are aware of it, this will be easier to explain.

"I do not favor my cousin, Miss Elizabeth, and Anne does not favor me. Anne has not told me, but I do not believe she wishes to marry at all, for I do not think she has the strength to endure it. But as Lady Catherine will not be gainsaid, we decided many years ago that it would be better to avoid an argument. That decision, it seems, was flawed, for we had not anticipated my aunt's irrational desire to have her way.

"If you recall, Fitzwilliam and I departed Rosings suddenly."

"I do," replied Elizabeth. "At the parsonage, we all thought it unusual that you would have left without taking your leave." She paused as another thought came to her. "Your aunt canceled our engagement that night, much to Mr. Collins's chagrin."

Mr. Darcy nodded and grinned, though it contained little mirth. "I am not surprised. That day, my aunt nearly ambushed me with a new demand that I marry Anne. As a bludgeon to enforce my compliance, she threatened to make Georgiana's near misstep public knowledge."

Aghast, Elizabeth stared at the gentleman before her. "Lady Catherine threatened to make your sister's near ruination known to society?"

"She did." Mr. Darcy's jaw might have been chiseled from granite. "I left at once, refusing to stay in her house a moment longer. She has bombarded me with continued entreaties and threats since that day, growing ever more insistent."

"How can she be so callous?" demanded Elizabeth.

She understood Mr. Darcy's nervous energy and need to pace, for she felt like it herself at that moment. Had Lady Catherine been anywhere in the vicinity, Elizabeth was uncertain she could have restrained herself from giving the lady a piece of her mind on which to chew.

"What a reprehensible creature she is! I knew she was a domineering shrew the instant I made her acquaintance, but I never considered her capable of such willful and disgusting disregard for the feelings and wishes of others."

"Lady Catherine is capable of any manner of vile threats to get her way," replied Mr. Darcy. "This much has become clear, though we always knew of her selfish disdain for the feelings of others. The worst of this situation is that Wickham took word of his scheme to gain my sister's fortune to my aunt, hoping to extort ready funds."

"So *that* is how she discovered it!"

Mr. Darcy nodded and said: "But my aunt is miserly, and Wickham did not gain nearly as much as he hoped. Regardless, he has none of it now, for we have dealt with him and relieved him of his ill-gotten gains."

It was difficult to understand, for she could not comprehend those who would go to such lengths to ensure their will reigned supreme. Even Lydia, selfish as she was, would not stoop to such depravity as this. What a woman Lady Catherine was! Elizabeth had never been so sorry for Charlotte as she was now, for to live under the thumb of such an odious woman could not be agreeable at all!

"This still does not explain everything, Mr. Darcy." Elizabeth searched the gentleman's eyes, trying to understand him. "How does this lead to your recent behavior?"

The gentleman's behavior was now more hesitant than Elizabeth had ever seen from him, for he turned away, running his hand through his hair yet again. He stood in indecision for a moment, wondering what he should say. The tension was nigh overwhelming, tempting Elizabeth to scream at him, to demand he simply tell her what he would have of her. But she held to her calm like the branch of a tree in a flood and waited for him to speak.

"I apologize if I have misled you, Miss Elizabeth," replied he after a moment. "I can understand if my actions have confused you. It seems I have botched this, and I give you my apologies for not being more open."

Elizabeth's heart went out to him, but the gentleman had not finished speaking.

"When Fitzwilliam and I returned to London, we considered the matter, trying to determine what we could do about the situation. During our discussions, we decided that Lady Catherine would lose her leverage if I were already married. I cannot marry *two* women."

All at once, the implications became clear to Elizabeth. "You wish to marry me?" Her question came out as little more than a squeak.

"I do, and quickly," replied Mr. Darcy. "Only yesterday I received another letter from Lady Catherine in which she informed me that she would act soon if I did not agree to her demands."

"But it is all so sudden! Only two weeks ago, I thought you looked at me only to catalog my faults. I did not like you much."

The ghost of a smile settled over his features. "Yes, I deduced that from Fitzwilliam's account of his meeting with you that day on the grounds of Rosings."

"And yet you thought I would be a good wife to you? I can hardly comprehend it."

Mr. Darcy's attitude again changed. He approached closer and knelt on one knee, taking one of her hands in his. The look he directed at her was earnest, as if he were baring his whole soul to her scrutiny.

"First, let me inform you that no man looks on a woman as much as I have looked on you for no other reason than to find a flaw, Miss Elizabeth. It was early in our acquaintance when I first found myself drawn to you, and the fascination has only increased in time."

The gentleman chuckled, a hint of nervousness contained therein, and added: "Do you know I entertained the thought of proposing to you the evening my aunt made her reprehensible demand?"

"How could you have managed it?" asked Elizabeth, curious despite the seriousness of the conversation. "Rosings would not have been conducive to such a discussion, and I had determined not to go before the message arrived from your aunt, canceling the evening."

"Perhaps I would have slipped away," replied Mr. Darcy. "I did not say it was a *good* notion, Miss Elizabeth; only that I had considered it. Now, of course, I understand it is better that I was prevented, for nothing good would have come of a proposal that evening."

"With that, I cannot but agree," said Elizabeth with a tentative smile.

Then another thought occurred to her. "Lady Catherine suspected your partiality!"

"She did?" demanded Mr. Darcy. "What did she say to you?"

Elizabeth explained Lady Catherine's visit, the questions she had asked, and the results which had puzzled her ever since. In particular, he inquired minutely into Elizabeth's responses and whether she had satisfied Lady Catherine with her answers.

"You did not promise you would not marry me," concluded Mr. Darcy when she had explained all.

For the first time, she understood why this would be of great import to him, given the tenor of their discussion. "No, I did not. Charlotte asked me the same question, but she has always suspected your interest in me. It appears my friend was more observant than I in this instance."

"And I am relieved you put Lady Catherine off without giving in to her demand. I could not, in good conscience, have asked you to break a promise you had so faithfully given."

"In truth," replied Elizabeth, "I would have considered it a trifle if I *had* given it. I certainly did not think her concerns had any merit, for, at that time, I had no notion of your interest."

Mr. Darcy fixed her with one of those looks, one which spoke to the utter seriousness of his intentions. Against her will, Elizabeth felt her stomach flipping in her midsection; for the first time, she wondered what it would be like to be the subject of this man's admiration. Or perhaps she already knew, as she knew by his testimony that he would not have resolved on her to this extent had he not already harbored an interest in her.

"It is much worse than that, Miss Elizabeth," said he, his voice quiet, yet intense. "For I have come to understand my feelings throughout this business, and they have far exceeded what I thought. If I had presented myself to you that evening in Hunsford, I would have approached, certain of my success. After all, what woman would reject me when I have so much to offer?

"In that, I deluded myself, for your feelings for me have become clear. If I would have you as a wife, I must approach you as a man approaches a woman, make you love me as I love you. I focused all my thought on what *I* would gain, not what I must do to win you. For that reason, I am glad the opportunity did not present itself, for I suspect it would have ended in disaster."

"With that, I cannot disagree," murmured Elizabeth. Then she settled a long look on him. "You love me?"

"I do," replied he. "I anticipate you will make me love you even more if you accept me, throughout all the years of our lives. But I do so now, and I humbly beg you to consent to be my wife."

While Elizabeth understood Mr. Darcy's nervousness would grow in his breast if she delayed, she could not help it. Even knowing Charlotte's opinion, she had not believed Mr. Darcy would make her this compliment. Again, she had been wrong. Spectacularly so.

The notion that she loved this man was ludicrous. She had disliked him not long ago. Did she still dislike him? No, she did not—that much was no less than obvious, absurd to even consider it. But love could not come into the equation yet, for there was still much about him she did not know.

The question then became, could she accept him if she did not love him? The pact she had with Jane had promised she would not accept any marriage proposal unless she loved the man who paid her the compliment of a proposal. It had been a simple decision to reject Mr. Collins, for love was so far beyond the range of possibilities of what she could feel for him. Could she dismiss Mr. Darcy's heartfelt proposal so callously?

It seemed the true heart of the matter was whether she thought she *could* love Mr. Darcy. But the answer to that question escaped her. How could she know? As she thought about it, clarity would not come, for the answer was beyond her at the moment. As important, however, was her knowledge that he loved and esteemed her, and his respect was strong, given his words to her that morning. Even if she never came to love him, his love for her would sustain her, and she would never end like her mother, slighted and despised by her husband. And once she knew this, Elizabeth's answer was easy.

"Yes, Mr. Darcy. I will marry you."

CHAPTER XI

For the briefest moment, Darcy did not understand her. Almost convinced as he was that she would refuse him, it seemed fantasy to hear her acceptance. Then the import of her reply pierced his consciousness, and he could not help the broad grin that came over his face.

"Thank you, Miss Elizabeth," said he, bending over to bestow a tender kiss on the hand he still held in his grasp. "You have my solemn word that I will do my utmost to ensure you *never* regret the trust you have placed in me."

Miss Elizabeth searched his eyes, looking for confirmation of the truth of his promise. Then she returned his smile and said: "I believe you, Mr. Darcy."

She paused, and a blush came over her face, turning her cheeks a delightful rosy hue. Ducking her head, she presented the image of a shy maiden. Given how confident this woman had always been in his company, Darcy was delighted to see it.

"This is all so new," said she, her voice much softer than usual. Then she met his eyes again, and he could read the trepidation. "And you wish to marry with such haste."

"It is, unfortunately, necessary. While I might wish to make love to you in the proper way, circumstances will not allow it, for it is imperative to take Lady Catherine's leverage from her at once." Darcy paused and smiled. "Therefore, you must allow me to make love to you after we are married, for I would not have you unhappy in our marriage."

Miss Elizabeth returned his smile, but it soon gave way to a frown. "I must wonder about your aunt, sir. Surely a woman willing to ruin her niece would not allow the impossibility of her designs once we are married to keep her from her purpose. Will she not still act out of spite?"

Darcy could not help but acknowledge her point. "It is possible, Miss Elizabeth, for Fitzwilliam made that same point. Yet, I cannot believe my aunt so lost to all common decency and sense that she would persist when she has no more hope of prevailing."

Another thought occurred to him, and he added: "I expect she will break with me over this, but to be honest, I cannot count that much of a loss."

"You will forgive me if I hope we will be in her company but seldom regardless of what happens."

"I cannot blame you at all, for that is my wish as well."

She smiled and nodded, then her thoughts turned to the practicalities. "We should speak of how we will move forward."

Darcy agreed. "First, I must solicit your father's permission. Do you suppose he will protest?"

An awful thought came over Darcy, for he had not considered the possibility of opposition in that quarter. Suddenly, he could not help but wonder if she would agree to go to Gretna Green with him.

"Papa will not object if I convince him of my desire to marry you." Miss Elizabeth gave him an impish smile. "That will not prevent him from making sport with you and having his fun."

Darcy was still not well acquainted with Mr. Bennet, but what he knew of the man suggested he had a quixotic sense of humor. "Excuse me, but you are not of age?"

"Not until July, Mr. Darcy," confirmed she.

For the first time, Darcy realized just how young she was. She had always given the impression of such worldly knowledge, such familiarity with the nature of the world and its people that it had simply never occurred to him. Yet, here she was, bravely accepting his proposal when she must believe she was not well enough acquainted with him to know whether she could love him, whether they would even suit. It humbled Darcy to witness her bravery. He resolved even more firmly to see to her happiness in life, and even more still, to alleviate her fears as best he could before they reached the altar, even though need limited their time.

"Furthermore, Mr. Darcy," said she, "you should know my mother will not appreciate such a brief engagement."

"Oh?" asked Darcy, uncertain of her meaning. "I assume you speak of more than the haste of our planned nuptials."

"I will be the first of her daughters to marry," replied she. "And you are a prominent man. She will wish to hold a celebration the likes of which will be spoken of for years after the event."

That was so like Mrs. Bennet that Darcy could not halt the chuckle that escaped his lips. Miss Elizabeth saw the humor in it, for she joined his mirth.

"That will be unfortunate," said Darcy. "But it cannot be helped. Do you suppose obtaining such a son-in-law will heal her bruised pride?"

Miss Elizabeth grinned. "Perhaps it will, though I will warn you that such hubris as this will not serve you well with me, sir."

"I promise, I shall be the very soul of humility."

They laughed together, delighting Darcy all over again. Then she turned serious once more.

"What will my neighbors say?"

"I have given this some thought, Miss Elizabeth." Darcy took a deep breath, wondering if she would find his idea palatable. "It was my thought that we should claim an engagement since we met in Kent. That will make our engagement a matter of over a month, rather than only a week."

She cocked her head to the side and regarded him seriously. "That will ease some of the problems of a hasty engagement."

"And when they see you are not increasing early in our marriage, that should do the rest."

Miss Elizabeth blushed at the implication, but she continued bravely: "Then why did we not announce it when I returned from Kent?"

"Because," replied Darcy, "I am an aloof and private man, a wealthy man who must have his way."

"It is not perfect," said she.

"No, but I think it will suffice."

She nodded, though he could see she remained unconvinced. "I suppose it must."

"Then shall we return to your home? I have a great desire to ensure your father sanctions our engagement as soon as may be."

With a smile, she agreed and rose, accepting his arm, and guiding him along the path toward her home, his horse, which had stood nearby unnoticed throughout their conversation, following behind. It surprised Darcy to note that more than an hour had passed. It was well, for he was reasonably assured they would not arrive before her family arose.

The family was in evidence when they arrived, a murmur of voices from the sitting-room reaching their ears. Darcy pushed such thoughts away, wishing to concentrate his attention on what was to come with Mr. Bennet. They doffed their outerwear and left it in the maid's care, Miss Elizabeth leading him into the house. Down the hall and to the left stood a sturdy oak door, one he knew led to Mr. Bennet's sanctum.

He stopped her with a hand on her arm and noted her uncertain look as she turned to him. Darcy smiled to reassure her. "I shall persuade him, Miss Elizabeth."

"I suspect *I* shall need to persuade him, Mr. Darcy. He will not be easy until he knows that this is what I wish."

Darcy nodded. "Then I shall allow you to make your case to him, while I make mine. He will not be in doubt of my wishes—this I vow to you."

Miss Elizabeth nodded and gestured at the door, a clear invitation for him to approach her father alone. Then with a smile, she turned away and climbed the stairs, no doubt to ensure her appearance was acceptable before she joined her mother and sisters. Darcy might have told her that she was no less than beautiful, but he allowed himself the simple pleasure of watching her until she disappeared up the stairs before he turned to the forbidding obstruction before him. The occupant responded to his staccato rap at once, and Darcy lost no time in stepping into the room.

The first thing he noted was what he had always seen when he entered—it was the room of a learned man. There was not a bare wall in the room, for bookshelves filled every available. And they were not empty, for the occupant made good use of them, such that Darcy could hardly see an empty space. On the far side of the room behind the desk was a large bank of windows looking out on the rear of the estate, the trees in the distance beginning to show their summer greenery. The desk was large and solid, made from cherry wood, unless Darcy missed his guess, a fine piece of furniture for a modest gentleman.

The man himself looked up from the book he held in his hand as

Darcy entered the room, an expression of mild interest turning to surprise when he recognized Darcy. At once he laid his book on the desk and stood.

"Mr. Darcy," said he, making his way around with hand extended. "Welcome, sir. You will forgive me if I express surprise, for I had not expected you to appear at my home so early."

"Not at all, Mr. Bennet," said Darcy. "I apologize for disturbing you this morning, but there is a matter of some importance I must discuss with you."

"Then, by all means, sit," said Mr. Bennet. "I was doing nothing important—merely whiling away a few moments before I must wrestle with the estate ledgers. It is a task that I singularly detest, you understand."

Darcy caught the man's ironic tone and chuckled. "I cannot think of a man who enjoys it, but it is a necessary evil, for one must understand the state of one's finances."

"Especially when one's wife routinely strives to exceed one's income."

It was not the first time Mr. Bennet had made such comments in Darcy's hearing, and he took no notice of it, instead focusing his attention on what he must tell Mr. Bennet. The gentleman invited him to sit, asked after his preference, and when Darcy declined his offer of refreshment, clasped his hands in front of him on his desk.

"Then how may I be of assistance?"

Darcy took in a calming breath, one he attempted to be as unnoticeable as he could. Then he looked Mr. Bennet in the eye and said: "I have come this morning, Mr. Bennet, to ask for your permission and blessing for the hand of your daughter."

The gentleman's eyebrows climbed his forehead. "That *is* a surprise, sir. But I would recommend you specify *which* daughter, for I *do* have five."

The comment might have been designed to ease the sudden tension between them. If it was, it certainly served its purpose, for Darcy chuckled, thinking it was an excellent example of this man's sense of humor.

"Though I am certain you already know, I am referring to Miss Elizabeth."

Mr. Bennet nodded, confirming his suspicions, and leaned back in his chair, considering Darcy while he fingered his pocket watch. "I *had* seen something of your improved relations, but this is beyond anything I might have considered. It seems my wife was correct, sir, which is itself an interesting development. She has been certain many times that some man or another favored one of her daughters; this is the first time one of *them* has ever been of a like mind."

Darcy chuckled at the man's jest. "Well, I *am* of a like mind, sir. Now that I have had some months to consider it, I have realized that it is unfathomable I might have resisted her appeal. You have sired an excellent woman, Mr. Bennet, though I am certain you already know it."

For a long moment, Mr. Bennet regarded him, perhaps attempting to judge the sincerity of Darcy's comment. Darcy was not afraid of his scrutiny, for he meant every word. Mr. Bennet seemed to come to the same conclusion, for he nodded to himself.

"I certainly cannot disagree with that assessment, Mr. Darcy. I have long considered my second eldest daughter the best woman of my acquaintance." The man smiled and added: "My other girls are all comely, though their characters contain varying degrees of flaws. I am fond of them all, though I am not blind to the fact that the only one who compares with Elizabeth is Jane."

"I believe, sir, that Bingley would disagree with that sentiment. We may allow him to continue in his delusion."

Mr. Bennet replied with a hearty laugh, and Darcy felt all would be well. Then again, he had yet to inform Mr. Bennet *when* he wished to meet his daughter at the altar.

"Very well," said the man. "I presume you have already proposed?"

"I have," confirmed Darcy. "We met this morning on your estate, and I seized the opportunity to ask for her hand."

Darcy fell silent, considering what he should say to this man. What he had discussed with Miss Elizabeth was of a sensitive nature, information he did not wish to make its way to the gossips of society. On the other hand, Darcy trusted Mr. Bennet, for while the man had a sardonic streak and did not control his family to the extent Darcy thought wise, he had always known Mr. Bennet was no telltale. He could trust the man with the information.

"There are several matters of which you are not aware, Mr. Bennet," said Darcy aloud, focusing his attention back on the other man. "There is a need to marry quickly, though not the reason which must have occurred to you."

The paleness that had suddenly come over Mr. Bennet's face receded, and he breathed out an explosive breath. "I wish, Mr. Darcy, that you would take care for my nerves. One day, when you have daughters of your own, you will understand."

Mr. Bennet peered at him and asked: "How soon?"

"Within a week or so," replied Darcy. "I dare not delay any longer."

The man's eyebrows seemed especially mobile that morning, for once again they climbed into his hairline. "That *is* precipitous. Perhaps you should explain your reasons for a quick marriage that do not involve my Lizzy's virtue."

With a nod, Darcy recounted the same tale he had told Miss Elizabeth, though he kept his account brief. Mr. Bennet, he noted, was not one to hide his reactions, for his disgust for Lady Catherine and Wickham, his satisfaction at the way Darcy had handled the latter, and his amusement at Darcy's plan to foil his aunt's intrigues were all plain on his countenance. When Darcy had finished, Mr. Bennet gave the appearance of thought and did not respond for several moments after.

"If I am honest with you," said Mr. Bennet at length, "I agree with Lizzy's assessment—if your aunt is willing to go so far as to expose your sister's transgression to compel you, she is almost certainly vindictive enough to publish it out of spite."

"That is possible," conceded Darcy.

"There is more to this than you have said, sir." Mr. Bennet regarded Darcy, his face now unreadable. "I suspect you have used this as a convenient excuse to justify marrying my daughter, a woman who is, after all, not of your level in society, regardless of her character."

"I shall not attempt to deceive you," replied Darcy. "There were many objections to overcome, and I shall not scruple to suggest I did not consider them at length. But I had also determined to propose to your daughter before Lady Catherine demanded my capitulation. And I truly believe she will desist when there is no more chance of coercing me, though there is little chance of our connection surviving."

Mr. Bennet released a sardonic laugh. "If you will pardon me, that seems like no great loss."

"I cannot agree more."

"Then the last matter of which to concern myself is for Lizzy's happiness. Given her character, I cannot but suppose you are aware of her previous opinion of you."

"In Kent, I learned something of it. Her opinion has improved."

"But it has not changed enough to render her in love with you." Mr. Bennet smiled. "Many accuse me of neglect to my family, and in some respects, they are not incorrect. But I know more than they suspect, including Jane and Elizabeth's pact to marry for nothing less than love. It is a large reason why I refused my fool cousin's hapless request for her hand, though I cannot imagine I might have given my consent if I had remained ignorant."

The way Mr. Bennet watched him made it obvious he was trying to provoke a reaction. "And I am grateful you did, Mr. Bennet. Marrying your daughter to such a specimen as your cousin would have been a travesty."

"I cannot agree more, sir. Then what have you to say on the matter of my daughter's happiness?"

"Only that I am determined to ensure she is always content," replied Darcy. "For my part, I adore Miss Elizabeth, for she is the finest woman of my acquaintance. While I have not provoked similar feelings in her, I am resolved to gain her affection. It may take a week, a month, or a year, but I shall have it if it is possible."

"Well, well," said Mr. Bennet. "I declare you are a man who just might succeed, though I suspect Lizzy will not make it easy for you."

"Perish the thought," murmured Darcy.

Diverted, Mr. Bennet chuckled and shook his head. "You know my daughter well, Mr. Darcy. She will not be content to be a society wife who follows her husband in everything, though she will not contradict you in public."

"Trust me, Mr. Bennet," replied Darcy, "if I wished to have a subservient wife, I might have married my cousin Anne, or even Miss Bingley."

"Yes, well, I understand why that was undesirable." Mr. Bennet eyed him and nodded. "Have you considered an explanation for the hasty nature of your nuptials?"

"We shall claim an engagement since we were in Kent together." Darcy paused, grinned, and added: "As for why we did not announce it upon our return, we can explain it as my eccentric desire for privacy as a wealthy man."

Mr. Bennet laughed. "Then let us speak of the specifics, for we must approach my wife with the details in hand, else she will press for a longer engagement. I will say, Darcy, that I am disappointed you and Bingley will take my most sensible daughters away and leave me with the silliest. But I suppose there is no help for it."

For the first time in her life, Elizabeth felt she understood her mother's nerves. The appeal of remaining in her room had almost kept her there, but she did not wish to allow Mr. Darcy to endure her mother's raptures without her. A corner of her mind still screamed at her, asking her what she was thinking to be accepting Mr. Darcy. But she could not back out now. It was done and there was no going back.

Fortunately, Mrs. Bennet saw nothing to give rise to any suspicion of Elizabeth's activities that morning, and for that she was grateful. The six women were ensconced together in the sitting-room, each with their amusements. Elizabeth nominally held a book in her hands, but she had not turned even a single page, and she could not have repeated the title, had she been asked. When the sounds of approaching feet reached her ears, she tensed, prompting a questioning look from Jane.

"Mr. Darcy!" exclaimed Mrs. Bennet when her husband entered the room, the gentleman following on his heels. "I had no notion you had come, sir. Has your excellent friend accompanied you?"

"Bingley is still at Netherfield," replied Mr. Darcy, "though I suspect he will come before long. I had a matter of business to discuss with your husband and came on ahead."

Impossible though it might have seemed, Mrs. Bennet did not understand the nature of Mr. Darcy's business. Elizabeth might have expected her flights of fancy to take wing at once, but she only regarded the gentleman with an uncomprehending stare.

"And what business do you suppose brought our neighbor here, Mrs. Bennet?" asked her husband. "It appears you do not recognize it yet, so I shall tell you. Unexpected it was, but Mr. Darcy approached me this morning for permission to marry your second eldest daughter. Do you know what I said?"

The first raptures had appeared on Mrs. Bennet's face, but her husband's tone dampened it, and she regarded him with suspicion. "I hope your response differed from the one you gave Mr. Collins."

Mr. Bennet chuckled and gave her a fond smile, something Elizabeth had rarely seen from him. Then he turned and regarded her, a hint of a question in his arched eyebrow. At that moment it was the hardest thing Elizabeth had ever done. But she gave him an imperceptible nod to satisfy him.

"There are differences between the two situations, Mrs. Bennet. With Mr. Collins, Lizzy rejected his proposal, and she was correct to do so. Time will tell if she has made a wise choice now, though Darcy has declared his esteem for her and his determination to have her as a wife. Either way, she has accepted him, and as she has given her consent, I have responded with mine."

"Mr. Darcy and Lizzy!" cried Lydia, her eyes wide as saucers. "Impossible!"

"It is not impossible, Lydia," said Elizabeth, hurrying to make her sentiments known. "Whatever happened between us in the past, we have settled it between us."

"And so, you should!" exclaimed an elated Mrs. Bennet.

"Oh, Mr. Darcy!" continued she, standing and approaching him. "I knew how it would be! My Lizzy is an excellent girl. It was only a matter of time before you saw how perfect she will be for you!"

"That she is, Mrs. Bennet. You should also know that we have been engaged since we met in Kent. But I wished to wait until she returned to make it official."

Such news could not help but shock her mother, but Mrs. Bennet pushed it to the side at once. "Well, I am glad you did. It shall be such a celebration as the neighborhood has never seen!"

A glance passed between Mr. Darcy and Mr. Bennet, the latter chuckling while the former appeared rueful. Mr. Darcy left it to Mr. Bennet to respond.

"For our family, I am certain no celebration could be more joyous. But as for the neighborhood, there will be little time for it. Mr. Darcy, you see, has informed me of his need to wed at once, and after listening to his reasons, I cannot but agree with him. Thus, the wedding will take place a week from today."

Stupefied, Mrs. Bennet gaped at her husband, wondering if he was jesting again at her expense. "What nonsense are you speaking, Mr. Bennet? They cannot marry in only a week's time! What will the neighbors say?"

"Whatever they say, it will change nothing. We set the wedding date for next week. Mr. Darcy already purchased a common license, and I shall speak to the parson this afternoon."

The news about the license was new to Elizabeth, and she looked to Mr. Darcy, wondering at his presumption. The gentleman, likely aware of what her response would be, fixed her with a faintly apologetic look, and nodded, promising he would explain it to her. Mollified, but not yet satisfied, Elizabeth allowed the matter to rest for the moment.

"No, no, no," cried Mrs. Bennet. "They cannot possibly marry before August. Michaelmas would be better, for a fete such as this requires careful planning."

"And yet, there is little choice," said Mr. Darcy. "I apologize, Madam, for the fault is mine. I cannot speak more plainly, but there are excellent reasons for the haste by which we must marry. There is no stain on your daughter, for we have kept ourselves under good regulation. But the fact remains that we must marry as soon as may be arranged."

Mrs. Bennet regarded him, a frown suggesting she was deep in thought. Elizabeth was convinced she would protest, but it appeared Mr. Darcy had persuaded her, for she nodded.

"Then we must begin at once. I have no notion of how we can plan your breakfast in naught but a week, but I shall attempt it."

"Thank you, Mrs. Bennet," replied Mr. Darcy. "I know how sudden this is. I appreciate the imposition and know you will work miracles in making it a memorable occasion for your daughter."

Mrs. Bennet preened at his praise.

"Now, however, I must return to Netherfield to apprise my family, for I did not wish to inform them of my engagement until your husband gave his sanction. Miss Elizabeth, will you walk me to the door?"

Elizabeth agreed at once, rising to take his arm while ignoring the chatter of her sisters. They passed through the door and the vestibule, where Mr. Darcy gathered his hat and gloves from the waiting maid, and then made their way out of doors.

"It appears I should have spoken of this," said Mr. Darcy, turning to her when they were standing on the portico. "I purchased a common license in London in the hope you would accept me. I knew there would be little time to return to London if I persuaded you."

Elizabeth nodded, knowing of his careful nature. "I understand, Mr. Darcy. It *was* a surprise, but your foresight was well judged."

Mr. Darcy smiled and grasped her hand. "Please allow me to thank you again, Miss Elizabeth. Though it may appear my aunt's actions have forced me to this, I wish to have you for a wife and anticipate our union very much."

"It is still a shock," replied Elizabeth. "But I believe I will become accustomed to it before long."

"That is well," said the gentleman. "I shall return with my family and Bingley when I have explained the morning's events to them. Until then."

Bowing, Mr. Darcy kissed the back of her hand and strode away. A moment later, he was astride his horse, cantering away from her toward Netherfield. Elizabeth might have stood there watching until she lost sight of him, but her mother proved her determination to make what she could of the time she had been given.

"Lizzy! Come here at once, for we must begin planning!"

CHAPTER XII

"*W*hat do you wish to tell us, Mr. Darcy?"

As he regarded Miss Bingley, who had spoken, Darcy reflected that he little wished to say *anything* to her. The nature of her sneering comment, the way her eyes raked over him in derision informed Darcy that she was not happy with the way this visit had gone. And yet, Darcy was unmoved, for he had never given Miss Bingley even the hint of encouragement her every action suggested. He would inform all his family of his engagement without her presence if he could manage such a feat. As it was, there was little enough he could do but announce it unless he wished to create a scene. Seeing her immediate reaction to the knowledge of his engagement would be its own recompense, so he forged ahead.

"Georgiana, Fitzwilliam," said he, nodding to his two family members, though his warm smile at Bingley informed him how welcome he was too, "it is my distinct pleasure to inform you that I have spoken to Miss Elizabeth, and we agreed it is time to reveal our secret. We have agreed to marry and are now ready to announce our engagement to the world."

Georgiana leaped to her feet and threw herself into his arms, babbling her excitement, while Fitzwilliam and Bingley stepped forward to offer their congratulations with hands extended and hearty slaps on his back. To expect Miss Bingley to remain silent at the dissolution of whatever dreams she possessed was beyond impossible, and after a moment of stupefied shock, she did not hesitate to make her opinion known.

"Engaged?" It was nearly a shriek, a match for the rage that descended over her face. "What a jester you are, Mr. Darcy! We are all familiar with your opinion of *Eliza Bennet*."

It did not surprise Darcy when the woman affected disbelief. But Darcy was not of a mind to allow her to persist.

"Indeed, you are incorrect, Miss Bingley," replied Darcy. "If you recall, it was not a week after first making her acquaintance when I first mentioned my attraction to her. To you, as I recall, at Sir William's party, when I spoke of her fine eyes."

Miss Bingley snorted. "And it was not long before that when you said: 'I should as soon call her mother a wit.'"

"Perhaps I did," replied Darcy, unwilling to give an inch. "I spoke wrongly then. I had barely looked at her and was unqualified to make such a judgment. I have learned since then what utter folly it was to speak such falsehoods."

"The truth, rather," snapped she. "Miss Eliza Bennet is nothing out of the common way. Indeed, sir, I must wonder how you have come to this end, for before we came to this miserable community, you were discerning and discriminating. And now you allow your sister to associate with the worst hoydens and propose to tie yourself to a family that should not show its face in polite society."

"That is enough, Caroline," growled Bingley, his voice unyielding. "Whatever you think of Darcy's choice, it is *his* choice. You have no right to disparage Miss Elizabeth. Hold your tongue!"

Miss Bingley wished to continue to argue; her obstinate jealousy informed Darcy that much. But whatever she meant to say, it appeared she did not wish to push her brother in this matter. As well she exercised restraint, for Darcy was not about to take much more of her insolence.

"Well, I say congratulations," said Fitzwilliam, giving Darcy another friendly slap on the back. "I always thought Miss Elizabeth was a rare woman. It is well you have snapped her up, for I have no doubt she would not remain unattached for long."

"And I am eager to gain five sisters!" exclaimed Georgiana in her excitement. "When will you gift me with these sisters, William?"

Darcy smiled at his sister for giving him the opening he needed, though unwittingly. "Very soon, my dear. Elizabeth and I have spoken, and we have agreed there is no reason to wait. Thus, we shall be married next week."

The only person in the room who understood the significance was Fitzwilliam, and he nodded his understanding, though Darcy saw his gaze go distant as if calculating the longest time they could wait and still be safe from Aunt Catherine's interference. While Georgiana and Bingley appeared surprised, the first response came from another, one from whom Darcy had heard more than enough.

"Next week, you say?" sneered Miss Bingley. "That is surprising. I suppose if I had recommended myself to as Miss Eliza Bennet appears to have done, I might have been more successful in inducing you to consider me. Then again, I have never had any desire to worm my way into your bedchamber, so I suppose it was a hopeless business from the start."

"You are correct in one aspect, Miss Bingley," said Darcy, speaking over Georgiana's gasp and Bingley's sudden fury at his sister. "It *was* a hopeless business from the start, but not for the reason you insinuate. The truth is I have no interest in marrying you, would never have offered for you even in the most extreme distress.

"As for your other disgusting insinuation, I shall not deign to offer a response. While you may scoff at the notion, I have offered for Miss Elizabeth for no other reason than pure inclination. Casting shade on her morality is laughable to anyone who knows her."

"Something Caroline knows very well herself," interjected Bingley. "Perhaps now, Caroline, you will confess the utter insufficiency of your pretensions and acknowledge what I have told you for years."

Miss Bingley appeared coldly furious, and when she opened her mouth, her brother neatly cut her off.

"If you have nothing constructive to say, I suggest you return to your room. Nothing will change Darcy's mind, and every insult you spew at Miss Elizabeth will make your situation worse."

Darcy might not have credited the woman's ability to make a sensible decision, but she surprised him by turning on her heel and marching from the room. When she was gone, Bingley turned back to Darcy.

"I apologize, my friend, for my sister's comments. While she had no right to say what she did, I must own that I am confused about the hurry too, especially as I might have expected Mrs. Bennet to wish to celebrate her first daughter's wedding with all the pomp she can muster."

With a grin, Darcy clasped his friend's shoulder. "And there you would be correct, Bingley, for Mrs. Bennet was not happy to know she will have so little time to plan. But it cannot be helped, though the need to marry swiftly is for reasons other than those your sister insinuated."

"I never would have thought anything different," replied Bingley with a firm nod. "To think *you* of all men could behave in such a manner as to make such things necessary is beyond contemplation."

Then Bingley strode to the sideboard and collected several glasses and a pair of decanters. He poured brandy for those remaining — sherry for Georgiana — and then proposed a toast.

"To Darcy and Miss Elizabeth. May they ever be happy in their union. And may I join him in that state of wedded bliss with Miss Bennet before long."

They laughed at Bingley's jest and drank, the mood festive. Perhaps in one part of that house, a thundercloud brooded, no doubt trying to conceive of a way Miss Elizabeth Bennet would not defeat her. As Darcy knew what she did not, that there was no way she could prevail, he refrained from considering her. Darcy hoped very much that from that point forward he would be but little in her company.

Later that day, Darcy found himself involved in a most uncomfortable conversation, and one he had not thought to have. The matter of why he was marrying Miss Elizabeth with such haste had not seemed to concern his sister in the slightest; she had fixed her attention on the benefit of having five new sisters to the exclusion of all other considerations. That was important to her, not the timing of when she would receive these new sisters. Fitzwilliam's opinion was not aligned with Darcy's.

"She needs to know, Darcy," said he, his typical bluntness in his short answer. "You are marrying Miss Elizabeth with what many will call unseemly haste, and part of the blame is Georgiana's for her actions last year. Of more importance, Lady Catherine will eventually learn of this and will not hesitate to come here. If you think Georgiana will not learn of it, you are fooling yourself."

"I would not cause her undue distress, Fitzwilliam," replied Darcy with a frown. "You know she will blame herself."

"A little blame will do her no harm," said Fitzwilliam. "Our Georgiana has learned and grown much this past year, and yet she behaved foolishly. She can withstand the truth of the predicament in which you find yourself."

While Darcy did not agree with his cousin, he capitulated, knowing that Fitzwilliam was capable of insisting when he thought he was right. Thus, Darcy asked Bingley for the use of his study—the door was thick and heavy, and would prevent any eavesdropping, should any decide to eavesdrop. When they led her into the room, they explained the events of the past few weeks. Needless to say, Georgiana was distressed.

"Oh, Brother," said she, tears rolling down her cheeks, "I had no notion Aunt Catherine made such despicable threats against me. How can I ever make it up to you? I do not wish you to marry simply to protect me and prevent Lady Catherine from making my misstep known."

"Georgiana, my dear," said Darcy, leaning forward to clasp her hand, "do not suppose that I mean to marry Elizabeth for only that reason."

His sister's eyes found his own, looking to determine the truth of his statement. Darcy smiled at her, informing her through the openness of his feelings for her and Elizabeth, the two most important ladies in his life.

"I have long felt an attraction to her, and for nearly as long, I have loved her with all my heart. It will not surprise you when I own that I delayed due to concerns for her position in society relative to our own?"

"If you will pardon me, Brother," said Georgiana, "I care little for what society thinks, and I suspect you are equally indifferent."

"I have learned that I am," confirmed Darcy. "But it took me several months before I acknowledged it, and this is the result."

"Then the haste is because of your desire to protect me?"

"It is," replied Darcy.

He caught sight of Fitzwilliam, who was watching them, his mien demanding that Darcy tell her all. This was perhaps the easiest portion to share, for if matters went sideways, it would be Darcy's fault that Lady Catherine would betray her secret to society.

"There is also a possibility of danger," said Darcy, drawing Georgiana's eyes to him again—he suspected she had returned to the pleasant thoughts of so many sisters to enliven her days. "Though I have acted to remove all possibility of our aunt forcing me to marry Anne, there is a distinct possibility that she might still reveal what she knows in a fit of vindictive revenge."

Georgiana's brow tightened as she considered this. In the end, she responded much as Darcy might have expected.

"But my coming out is at least two years away. By that time, much of whatever gossip she causes will have died away."

Darcy shared a look with Fitzwilliam, but his cousin responded. "It may. Your introduction will return it to the minds of our peers, but I cannot believe it would last long."

"I do not care," said Georgiana with a shake of her head. "If I must suffer a little for my foolishness, then it is my own doing. The price to pay to buy our happiness will be well worth it." She paused and grinned at Darcy. "Besides, if Aunt Catherine behaves in so reprehensible a fashion, we may take the opportunity to cut her from our lives. I hope you will not blame me, Brother, if I declare that the thought of losing Aunt Catherine's society brings me little grief."

Fitzwilliam released a hearty guffaw, which Darcy echoed. "No, Georgiana, I do not blame you. The thought of losing Aunt Catherine's society is quite agreeable to me too."

"Then let us consider the matter settled," replied she. "Now, I wish to go to Longbourn at once, for I have a great desire to see my new sister. And her mother will require assistance with wedding preparations!"

As his sister continued to chatter about the expected delights of having a brother married and new sisters, not to mention wedding preparations, Darcy could not help but note how resilient she seemed to have become. Darcy was not eager for the preparations, but the matter of the wedding was now a lifeline, a definite line in the sand beyond which he could be easy from any thought of Aunt Catherine's coercion. He would endure all that led to that day, for he knew it would bring him the greatest of happiness.

"Well, Lizzy," said her father when Mrs. Bennet finally released Elizabeth from her incessant talk of wedding preparations, "I never would have guessed this morning that I would have an engaged daughter before the end of the day. If I had considered such a thing, I would have thought it would be Jane. Yet here we are."

"Yes, we are, Papa," replied Elizabeth in a soft voice. "I might never have guessed it myself."

Mr. Bennet regarded her, a hint of his old sardonic outlook on life mixed with his ever-present concern for her, his favorite daughter. Elizabeth was not blind to his scrutiny, but for the moment she felt unequal to responding, or even meeting his gaze. Instead, she concentrated on the room in which they sat, the refuge her father had relied on most of his married life, which had also been a retreat for her on more occasions than she could count. Soon, she would leave his home for her own, and her connection to this room would be irrevocably strained, for it would never be as it once had been.

A movement caught her attention, and she fixed her gaze on her father, noting how he had leaned forward, that he was regarding her with a seriousness she had rarely seen from him. They bought his blessing for their engagement with the knowledge that Elizabeth had given her consent to Mr. Darcy's proposal. But she knew he wished further reassurance of her reasons. Elizabeth could not think of grieving a beloved parent who had supported her all the days of her life.

"It *was* my choice, Papa," said Elizabeth, answering his unspoken question.

"Yes, that seems to be the case," mused her father. "What I do not yet understand is why. Did you not always swear to only marry a man you loved?"

"It is true that I do not love Mr. Darcy, Papa," said Elizabeth. "Yet."

One eyebrow arched in response to her statement. "Then you believe you will?"

"I understand the possibility, and I have determined to do all I can to find that state. And I know that Mr. Darcy wishes me to return his love."

"Well, having the devotion of a man of Mr. Darcy's mettle is not an insubstantial matter," replied her father. "If you will permit me, your acceptance was what the poets might call a leap of faith."

"In many ways, you are correct," replied Elizabeth. "I saw something in Mr. Darcy these past two weeks, Papa. He is not the cold, unfeeling man we all thought he was. Mr. Darcy feels deeply, and in many respects, I believe he struggles to express himself."

"I cannot disagree. That there was much more to Mr. Darcy than we thought I could see the moment he reappeared in Hertfordshire." Mr. Bennet gave her a wry smile. "Even if he was attempting to make love to us all, hoping to propose to you."

Elizabeth nodded but did not belabor the point. No one in the family outside this room would ever know why they were marrying with such haste—at least if Lady Catherine did not appear and inform them all, that was. What the lady would do, Elizabeth could not say, but she knew the scene would do no one involved any credit. She would almost certainly reference Elizabeth's conversation with her at Hunsford, but Elizabeth was not prepared to give up that point. Lady Catherine *had* asked for a promise, but Elizabeth had not given her one, not that the existence of a promise given in ignorance and dislike would have given her a moment's hesitation. Charlotte had been incorrect about that point.

"Well then, Lizzy," said Mr. Bennet, drawing her attention again, "what is done is done, and we can only hope for the best. For whatever it is worth, I believe you shall do well together, especially as you are both determined to make something of it. He is a good man and will do right by you—I would not have given my permission had I thought otherwise."

Smiling, Elizabeth rose and kissed his head, and departed the room. It had been a long day, and she was eager to find her bed. She had not, however, counted on the insistence of a most beloved sister, one who was not of a mind to allow a moment longer to pass without obtaining an explanation.

"Lizzy," said Jane, poking her head in through the open door not long after Elizabeth had entered herself. "Can I speak to you for a moment?"

Elizabeth smiled at her sister, even as she wondered at Jane's diffidence. They had long been accustomed to meeting in each other's rooms in the evenings to discuss the day's events or just enjoy their close relationship. With a pang, Elizabeth considered how her impending wedding must bring that practice to an end, for she would live with her husband and no longer be at liberty to indulge in such girlish practices.

Seeing her smile, Jane entered the room, situating herself gingerly on the edge of Elizabeth's bed, her gaze darting about the room as if she had never seen it before. Her eyes would not quite meet Elizabeth's, furthering her perplexity. Jane was acting strangely that evening—it was most unlike the sister she adored!

"What is it, Jane?"

At Elizabeth's prompting, Jane finally met her gaze, but what Elizabeth found within did not make her feel any better. Elizabeth had rarely seen Jane discomposed, and even when she was, she hid it well enough that only those who knew her best could see it—Elizabeth often had trouble herself. For Jane to be showing this much of her emotions must mean they were powerful, indeed!

"It is just . . . What I wish to say . . ."

Jane paused and struggled for the words. Finally, she gave a little cry, threw her hands into the air, and said: "I know not how to express myself, for there seems little enough for me to say."

"Perhaps you should just come out and say what you are thinking, Jane," replied Elizabeth, now completely confused. "It will be easier that way."

"I hardly think that will be conducive to harmony between us," muttered Jane.

"What do you mean?" asked Elizabeth, feeling the urge to gape.

"Why, only that you have secured the man you will marry with such apparent ease."

Had Elizabeth thought Jane's behavior shocked her before, what she felt now put that emotion to shame. The implications of Jane's word hit her like a stampeding horse, and she said: "Jane, are you jealous?"

Jane fixed her with such a look of crossness that Elizabeth felt like a naughty child facing a governess rather than a treasured companion. "What do you suppose, Lizzy? I have hoped and grieved and wished for Mr. Bingley to return to me, through many months of suspense. Yet Mr. Darcy comes here only three weeks ago, makes love to our family, and two weeks after you arrive you are engaged to him. Do I not have a reason for jealousy?"

The only thing Elizabeth could do was gape at her sister. Jane did not endure it for long, for she huffed and said: "You need not look at me so, Lizzy. I know how you consider me to be without fault, yet I possess the same failings as any other woman."

"I know you are not perfect, Jane," said Elizabeth. "But I never would have expected it of you, especially considering how Mr. Bingley appears eager to make you his wife as soon as may be. He will not be content to be long outdone by his friend."

A blush was Jane's response, and she turned away. For a long moment, she did not speak, and Elizabeth wondered if she would stand and flee the room. Then she turned back to Elizabeth and fixed her with a tremulous smile.

"That is the only reason I am not wild with envy, Lizzy, for Mr. Bingley has all but declared himself. But you must own that you have come to your resolution in a much more expeditious manner."

"How expeditious do you call it?" cried Elizabeth. "In October, the man I am to marry slighted me and I have despised him ever since. Then his greatest enemy saw my dislike and used it for his own ends, making a fool out of me. These past weeks have been the most humbling time of my life, Jane, and it was all my own doing."

"Oh, Lizzy!" exclaimed Jane, drawing Elizabeth into an embrace. "That is the real reason I wished to speak to you, for I am worried. Since October, you have not had a good word to say of Mr. Darcy, and yet you are now engaged to him. Though I will own to feeling jealous,

I am more concerned for your wellbeing. Will you not explain why you have agreed to marry him?"

Before coming to her room, Elizabeth had thought she had to keep the truth of her engagement between herself and her father. Now, however, she knew she could not keep Jane in suspense, for her dearest sister was entitled to know. Thus, Elizabeth drew Jane onto the bed beside her and told her the tale of the previous weeks, including what Mr. Darcy had told her, laying out her reasons for accepting Mr. Darcy, her hopes for the future, along with her fears.

And throughout that long evening, two beloved sisters, each other's closest confidantes, grew impossibly closer because of this shattering of the final barrier between them. As she lay drifting to sleep, having spent many long minutes assuring Jane of her belief it would all work out, Elizabeth found she felt much better about the situation. Jane was an excellent listener, providing a willing ear and an excellent sense of proper advice, without judging or questioning her motivations. Perhaps all *would* turn out well yet.

CHAPTER XIII

"*I*f I must visit another house or accept one more intrusive felicitation designed to elicit a confession of scandalous behavior, I believe I shall scream!"

Mr. Darcy looked at Elizabeth, his eyes twinkling with suppressed laughter. "Should I take note of this? By all accounts, *you* are the social part of our future union. If you are not, then I can alter my future expectations, and we may stay at Pemberley, for I have little interest in society."

While she attempted a glare at the gentleman, his mirth was infectious, sweeping Elizabeth along in its current. There was something ridiculous about the whole situation, and Elizabeth could not help but acknowledge it.

"I apologize, my dear," said Mr. Darcy when Elizabeth paused to consider their situation. "Though I have done my best to help ease the burden, it appears you have endured much more than I might have thought."

"It is nothing," replied Elizabeth. "I might never have dreamed how indefatigable my mother can be, even given my years of experience with her character. Had our engagement proceeded normally, we might have endured visits to the neighborhood and talk of wedding preparations over the space of several months."

"And yet, our haste has condensed into only a week," observed he.

"Much to my chagrin."

Mr. Darcy regarded her for a long moment. "Yes, I can see it has been trying on your patience. To own the truth, I have liked it less than you."

"You have not given the appearance of impatience," noted Elizabeth, fixing the gentleman with a quizzical look.

"Ah, but it is incumbent upon me to endure it without complaint." The gentleman grinned and added: "After all, am I not the cause for *your* current discomfort? The least I can do is endure it silently and attempt to bear you up when your strength is waning."

Statements like this one no longer surprised Elizabeth, for she had become accustomed to this side of Mr. Darcy, a side she had never seen. The image of Mr. Darcy she had set in her mind had been that of a dour man, one who had no time or patience for social niceties, a man for whom spending many hours in the sitting-rooms of country estates would be the cruelest punishment.

And yet, the man had shown himself adept at knowing when Elizabeth needed relief, had acted with her comfort foremost in his mind. Throughout the long hours in which her mother had shown her engaged daughter and her betrothed to every family in the neighborhood—and a few outside it!—she had seen no signs of intolerance, nothing of that colossal pride she had thought was his defining characteristic. Now the question of his forbearance was answered, for it was all for her!

Yet it was not, for underneath it all, Elizabeth realized that for perhaps the first time she had known him, Mr. Darcy was showing her his true self, uncolored by prejudice or any effort at remaining hidden. That Mr. Darcy was a good, conscientious, responsible man was a notion to which she was becoming accustomed. It boded well for their future felicity.

"Such constant attention *is* difficult to endure," said Mr. Darcy. Then the man gained a mischievous air as he added: "But I believe you are not looking at the advantages."

"Which are?" prompted Elizabeth, wondering if she should not inquire.

"Why, that we must only endure it for a week. Just think of the state we would be in if we faced several months of this wedding talk! I cannot imagine it would be agreeable to either of us!"

"Yes, you have a point," replied Elizabeth with a chuckle. "I can imagine the lavish preparations in which my mother might engage if we were engaged for months. By the time a month had passed, I might have been ready to make for Gretna Green!"

"That would be no difficulty for me. I might have suggested it in our current situation had I thought my plea had a chance of success."

"If you proposed it now, I cannot imagine I would not agree with alacrity."

They gaze at each other momentarily before their mirth came gushing out in torrents. Among the outcomes Elizabeth might have expected, laughing with her betrothed was *not* one she could have imagined. And yet, it appeared the greater part of her previous understanding must now give way to what she knew now. Mr. Darcy was not that great impenetrable wall she had thought he was. There were depths to the man that would take a lifetime to uncover.

"At least there have been few overt questions concerning our rush to the altar," said Elizabeth when their laughter had run its course. "Despite my earlier complaint."

"Did you expect anything different from your friends?" asked Mr. Darcy.

Elizabeth could only shrug. "This situation is beyond my experience. When I was a child, I remember rumors about a lady in the neighborhood. I do not even know if there was any validity in them. But the gossip about her was so vile and persistent, that it chased her from our midst. I was only a child, but I remember what they said about her."

"And you expected the same?" asked Mr. Darcy.

With a sigh, Elizabeth gave him a wan smile. "I did not know what to expect. That we will soon marry must have a mitigating effect on whatever notions they might have for the reason of our haste. At the very least, I expected comments, but there have been few enough of those, though of innuendo, there has been plenty."

Mr. Darcy regarded her gravely. "I cannot say you are incorrect to feel that way, Miss Elizabeth. I have seen gossip shred reputations in London, and for much less than the small missteps I have endeavored to hide."

"Yet, you have risked the knowledge of those missteps coming to society's attention by defying Lady Catherine."

"I have," said Mr. Darcy. At her level look, he nodded and said: "My actions are based as much on the desire to be bound to *you* as it is my need to avoid marriage to my cousin. But I would not have acted this way if I did not believe there is some hope of convincing Lady

Catherine to desist."

Elizabeth already knew this, but it still flattered her. It was a matter of some wonder that she had prompted the devotion of a man such as Mr. Darcy, a man who could have virtually any woman he wished. It was humbling and exhilarating at the same time. The possibility of a happy ending, of entering a marriage built on respect and esteem, and eventually love, never seemed higher than it did at that moment. Times like this were when Elizabeth's confidence was at its highest.

"What do you suppose Lady Catherine will do when she learns of our union?" asked Elizabeth to change the subject and overcome her sudden shyness.

Mr. Darcy could not hide the wince—in truth, Elizabeth felt little different. "Nothing good. At the very least, I cannot but think she will journey here at once to confront us." Mr. Darcy gave a mirthless chuckle. "I am expecting it, for I suspect her need to make her sentiments known to me will prevent her from spreading what she knows about town at the first opportunity."

"You mean to use that time to persuade her from acting."

"Yes," replied Mr. Darcy.

"But surely you do not mean for her to learn of our union through gossip."

"No, that would be disastrous," agreed Mr. Darcy. "Instead, I shall write a letter to her when we are wed. That way she will learn from me, and it will be too late for her to stop our wedding."

Elizabeth nodded, agreeing it was as workable a plan as any. "Then I shall steel myself against anything she might muster, for she will have many things to say to me. In particular, I have no doubt she will speak of our conversation before I left Kent."

"On the contrary, my dear Elizabeth," said Mr. Darcy, "I have no intention of allowing her to speak to you at all. This irrational pursuit of a marriage between my cousin and me has nothing to do with you. I have no intention of allowing her to abuse you in my presence."

"And yet, I am the one upsetting all her dreams of it coming to pass."

Mr. Darcy gave her a tender smile. "You are. But I would not marry Anne even if I had not met you. I simply would have gone about making my escape in another manner."

"Why, Mr. Darcy," said Elizabeth, feigning astonishment, "it is not my person alone that has led you to such drastic measures?"

"It most certainly is," replied Mr. Darcy. "But the desperation is not part of this situation, only a convenient outlet for its release."

Elizabeth grinned and nodded. "In some way, this whole matter reeks of cowardice, for a large and capable man like you to run in fear of your aunt is somehow diverting."

"Just remember that she is a dragon, Miss Elizabeth," replied Mr. Darcy, his light tone informing her he had seen her words for the jest they had been. "Lady Catherine has fangs enough to mortally wound any man. It is fortunate for me I can hide behind your skirts, for I know you will slay the dragon in my defense."

"That I will, Mr. Darcy. That I will."

If the preparations and Mrs. Bennet's intention to present her daughter and her betrothed to every gentle sitting-room south of Cambridge were not enough, soon another folly of a most acute kind made itself known to the Bennet family. Though Elizabeth had paid little attention to it, the news of the regiment's impending departure for their summer encampment had spread about the community like wildfire, leaving bereaved and bewildered girls in its wake. The most affected were Kitty and Lydia, to the surprise of no one who counted the girls as acquaintances.

"You care nothing for our plight!" accused Lydia of Elizabeth a few days before the departure. "Do you not know that our hearts are broken?"

"She can hardly misunderstand your devastation," replied Mr. Bennet from where he sat nearby perusing his newspaper. "You have informed the entire family every fifteen minutes since learning of it. Indeed, I believed I dreamt last night about how broken are your hearts!"

Lydia shot a hateful look at her father before her accusing glare returned to Elizabeth. It was a challenge Elizabeth did not hesitate to meet.

"You are correct, Lydia, for I find myself quite unperturbed by your desolation. Even if I cared for the officers at all, I have other matters with which to occupy myself."

"Your *wedding*," spat Lydia, her contempt writ large upon her brow. "To perhaps the most boring man alive!"

It was fortunate for Lydia that Mr. Darcy and his sister were not at Longbourn, for Elizabeth might have given Lydia a set down from which she would not soon recover. Not that she might have bothered, for there was another in the room that was now Mr. Darcy's most loyal champion. She would not stand for any daughter of hers maligning him.

"Be quiet, Lydia!" exclaimed Mrs. Bennet. "Your sister has made a fortunate alliance, and one which will throw you into the path of wealthy men of high society. You should be grateful for Lizzy's good fortune."

That Lydia did not agree could be seen in her scowl of annoyance and mutinous glare. Mercifully, the girl did not persist in speaking of Mr. Darcy, choosing instead to begin a new recitation of her many tribulations, one with which the entire company had become fatigued. When her father silenced her a few moments later, Lydia pulled her conspirator from the room, the sounds of the girls stomping up the stairs informing them all of their intent upon venting their sorrows in the privacy of Lydia's room.

Yet this did not last, for later that very same day a letter arrived for Lydia, and the girl could not hide its contents for a moment. Her excitement as she skipped into the room was only matched by Kitty's misery, not that Lydia gave any thought for her sister.

"Mama! Mama! You will never guess what this is!"

Mrs. Bennet regarded the paper brandished in Lydia's hand. "Not unless you stop long enough for me to read it."

But Lydia did not listen, and capered about the room, crowing her delight at the top of her lungs. "It is an invitation from Harriet Forster to join her in Brighton as her particular companion. I am to go to Brighton and remain in company with all the officers! Is that not a fine thing?"

It was clear to Elizabeth that Mrs. Bennet could not say whether it was a fine thing, for she watched her youngest daughter, a frown etched in the lines on her face. In times past, Mrs. Bennet might have joined in Lydia's exultations. Yet now that her second daughter had made such a fortunate alliance with a wealthy man, Mrs. Bennet's imagination was afire with thoughts of other such futures for all her daughters. Why should she accept the attention of some poor officer when a more illustrious match was in Lydia's future?

Mr. Darcy and Georgiana came soon after with Mr. Bingley and Colonel Fitzwilliam, and Lydia did not stint in demanding their congratulations for her good fortune. They gave it hesitantly, then Mr. Darcy made his way to Elizabeth for an explanation, and Georgiana to Kitty, where she assumed the responsibility of comforting the bereft girl. Mr. Bingley was, of course, with Jane, and nothing would move him from her side.

Thus, it went on, Lydia flitting from one subject to another, asking her mother about new clothes for her time in Brighton or teasing Kitty about her exclusion. Before long, Kitty's misery was acute, despite Georgiana's gentle coaxing, and Lydia's satisfaction had grown to nearly the size of her swelled head. Through it all, Elizabeth watched and wondered how her family's reputation would ever survive Lydia's presence in Brighton intact. And Elizabeth wondered if she could convince her father to forbid her permission to go.

"It is not necessary," said Mr. Darcy when Elizabeth observed this to her.

Elizabeth regarded him, wondering what he meant. "Do you not think she will ruin us all if she is allowed to go in all this state?"

"Perhaps she would surprise you," said Mr. Darcy. "Regardless, I do not think it is necessary to speak to your father. Look at him."

At Mr. Darcy's gesture, Elizabeth looked at her father, noting that while he appeared to be concentrating on the pages of his book, his eyes rarely moved along the lines of text. He appeared to be focused on his youngest daughter, and while few would have noted anything unusual in his eyes, Elizabeth detected a definite hint of displeasure. Mr. Bennet let Lydia go on for perhaps ten more minutes before he intervened.

"I must own to some astonishment," said Mr. Bennet during a brief lull in Lydia's celebration. He looked up from his book as if he just noticed something different in the room's atmosphere. "Has something happened to provoke such ecstasy?"

"Papa!" exclaimed Lydia. "Did you not hear me tell you all that I am to go to Brighton this summer?"

"I heard you," said Mr. Bennet, his wry tone portending some witticism. "I suspect there are people in Derby who are, at this moment, wondering whence the sounds of celebration assailing their ears originated. What you seem to have forgotten, Daughter, is that you require permission to go to Brighton."

"Oh, I know you will not prevent me, Papa," said the girl, her flippancy provoking a muscle to twitch in his jaw, not that she noticed anything. "I expect you will revel in the quiet in your home when I am gone."

"While you may have been correct in other times," corrected Mr. Bennet, "in this instance, your conviction is misplaced. I have no intention of allowing you to accept this invitation."

"Papa!" cried Lydia aghast.

"No, Lydia," replied Mr. Bennet with as much firmness as Elizabeth had ever heard from him. "You are yet fifteen, and Mrs. Forster is no fit chaperone, considering she is only a year or two older and is as silly as you are yourself. The knowledge that we did not know of the snake in our midst for so many months has made me more cautious. We would still have him if not for Darcy here. I shall not repay his courage by placing you in a situation in which you may do your utmost to ensure the Bennet family is forever spoken of in whispers."

"No, indeed!" exclaimed Mrs. Bennet. One look at her informed Elizabeth that her mother had caught the insinuation in her husband's words and was his firmest supporter. "Even if your father was of a mind to allow it, I would have argued against it, Lydia. Your sister is about to be married, and I would have you all present for the joyous occasion."

"But Mama—" whined Lydia.

"Not another word," said her mother. "The matter is closed."

It appeared her parents' united stance awakened the girl to the hopelessness of her situation, for she crossed her arms and threw herself into the sofa beside Georgiana, her pouting glares fixed upon them all. Now that she was not to be left behind, Kitty appeared easier—not to mention smug—and now Georgiana's efforts fixed on Lydia. It was clear she had as little success with the youngest Bennet sister as she had had with the elder.

"And that, as they say, is that," said Mr. Darcy quietly to Elizabeth.

Elizabeth nodded, though her focus was still on Lydia. "Perhaps we may make her disappointment easier to bear."

Mr. Darcy smiled and nodded, seeming to understand Elizabeth's inference. Thus, she turned and addressed her sisters.

"It will not be Brighton, Lydia, but perhaps you may travel this summer after all."

While Lydia's vexation did not cease, she turned to Elizabeth, curious as to her meaning.

"I am to be married and none of you have ever seen my new home." Elizabeth shrugged and gave a helpless laugh. "*I* have never seen my new home. I should like all my family to view it with me for the first time."

"Go to Pemberley?" demanded Lydia. "Are there officers there?"

Mr. Darcy coughed, hiding a laugh, Elizabeth had no doubt. "There are no officers unless we invite my cousin to join us, something I am loath to do, given how much of a leech he can be."

"Confess it, Darcy," said Fitzwilliam, "you enjoy it when I leech from you."

"Oh, that will make up for my missing Brighton," was Lydia's caustic reply, though she had nearly spent her irritation.

"Perhaps it will not," said Elizabeth. "But I should think you would wish to see a place you have never seen before. I am of a mind to invite all my sisters." She turned to Mr. Darcy. "If you concur."

"You are to be the mistress of my house, Elizabeth," replied Mr. Darcy. "As such, it is your prerogative to invite whomever you like. Would your entire family not like to join us?"

Mr. Darcy turned his attention and Mr. Bennet and said: "You have heard of the library at Pemberley, sir. Surely you would like to sample its delights."

"Careful, Darcy," replied Mr. Bennet. "If you invite me into that enchanting room, you may never be rid of me."

"I shall take that chance, sir," replied Mr. Darcy with a laugh. Then he returned his attention to Elizabeth. "And what of your aunt and uncle? I seem to remember something of a tour this summer. They could use Pemberley as a base from which to see whatever they wish in the area."

"Could you endure their children, sir?"

"It has been many years since there were children at Pemberley, but I suspect the estate will survive."

Moved, Elizabeth placed her hand on his arm and nodded her thanks. "I shall speak to Aunt Gardiner when she comes for our wedding and propose it. I cannot imagine they will refuse."

It was settled. It was not Lydia's wish of flirting with the officers. But Elizabeth supposed it was better than nothing in the girl's mind. And it just might save them all.

The day of Elizabeth's wedding finally dawned bright and clear, a warm late spring day that threatened to douse the land with glorious sunshine. It was an auspicious portent of Elizabeth's future life with the man to whom she was to be joined that day, a sign that she would attain all she had ever hoped. Perhaps it was silly to equate the weather of a single day with the success of a marriage, but it was on Elizabeth's mind, nonetheless.

"It is time to rise, Lizzy," said Mrs. Bennet as she bustled into Elizabeth's room that morning far earlier than Elizabeth had ever seen her mother stir from her bed before. "There is too much to be done before we must depart for the church to allow you to linger."

That her mother was busy chivvying Elizabeth out of bed, the daughter most likely to arise with the sun, was no less than ridiculous. Jane knew it too, for she stepped into the room on her mother's heels, looked to Elizabeth, and looked heavenward. Mirth on her lips,

Elizabeth threw back her coverlet and sat up, yawning the last of her fatigue away.

From that moment forward, she was the center of a whirlwind of activity. First, her mother had a bath drawn for her, and when she had bathed, the maid arrived to style her hair, her mother fussed with her locks, insisting they were to be done just so, after which she dressed in her wedding gown. It was a new and eye-opening experience for Elizabeth, for her mother had never been so attentive to her before, had never been so determined to ensure Elizabeth looked her best. And when her efforts were complete, she held Elizabeth at arms' length and inspected her.

"Perfect," said Mrs. Bennet, satisfaction in her tone. "You look particularly lovely this morning, Elizabeth. The force of your appearance will strike your lover dumb."

"Thank you, Mama," Elizabeth croaked, emotion clawing at her voice while tears stung at the corners of her eyes.

"It is the truth, Lizzy," said Jane. "I have never seen you looking so beautiful."

Feeling beautiful for the first time, even when compared with her lovely elder sister, Elizabeth nodded, unable to speak, and allowed them to lead her below stairs where her father waited. He too was effusive in his appreciation, though Elizabeth again could not respond. Soon the family departed for the church and Elizabeth's destiny, which she now found herself equal to the task of meeting.

The ceremony she supposed was much the same as any other performed in that church through the long years of its existence. Every such event was significant to those involved in it, and Elizabeth was no less moved than any other. The one dissenting opinion was Miss Bingley, who occupied the pew beside her brother, her face etched with cold fury. But Elizabeth ignored her, for she would not allow someone so wholly unconnected with her to ruin this day of all days. Another unexpected presence was that of Colonel Fitzwilliam's brother, the viscount, who had arrived the previous evening for his cousin's nuptials. The thought of meeting a member of the nobility did not daunt Elizabeth, but she put his presence to the side for the moment to concentrate on her wedding.

Then the ceremony was over, and those invited made their way to Longbourn for the wedding breakfast. Had Elizabeth not been involved with every minute detail, she might not have believed her mother could plan such a feast. Whatever else Mrs. Bennet was, the woman was a consummate hostess, which she showed in the variety of foods set out for the enjoyment of her guests. Mrs. Bennet was in her element, moving from one neighbor to the next, speaking of the satisfaction of having a daughter married and accepting the congratulations they offered. As Elizabeth was superfluous to this activity, she and her new husband mingled among their guests, their acceptance quieter, yet no less grateful.

Before the breakfast was fifteen minutes old, disaster struck. It began on the edge of consciousness, the sound of a heavy carriage rumbling over the driveway, accompanied by the crack of a whip. While these signs escaped Elizabeth's notice altogether, the sound of a loud voice in the entryway did not. Mr. Darcy looked up upon hearing it, much as Elizabeth did, and the man's countenance became a mixture of resignation and fury.

But before he could so much as move, the door opened, and a lady barged into the room, a servant trailing her. The lady's eyes fell like a bludgeon upon their guests, searching until she found Mr. Darcy. Then they narrowed, the rage showing in the veins running like fire in the whites of her eyes.

Lady Catherine de Bourgh had come.

CHAPTER XIV

"*H*ow dare you!"
Lady Catherine's forceful denunciation provoked a shocked Darcy into action. As he stepped forward to confront her, he noted the support of his cousins, Colonel Fitzwilliam's countenance was like a thunderhead while his elder brother was calm and rational, but no less angry with the woman. Together they converged on her, but Lady Catherine gave no sign that the three tall men approaching her gave her any pause.

"What is the meaning of this, Darcy?" demanded she in a voice saturated with hate. "You were to marry Anne. I warned you of the consequences if you did not do your duty, and yet I find you making merry with this *woman* against all common decency. Explain yourself!"

"As I informed you, Lady Catherine," snarled Darcy, keeping his tone low to keep control over himself, "I have and had no intention of bowing down to your ridiculous commands. My declaration when I departed Rosings is still in force—the Darcys of Pemberley will no longer acknowledge the de Bourghs of Rosings Park as connections."

The woman's eyes narrowed. "You could not be so insensible to the harm that will fall on you if you disobey me."

"And yet here we are. You are too late, Lady Catherine, for I am already bound to another. It would be best if you returned whence you came and cease to bedevil us."

A corona of fire ringed Lady Catherine's eyes, and Darcy knew her ladyship would strike him down had she the power to do so. Then someone else entered her field of vision and she turned to batter down on this new source of frustration with the hammer of her glare.

"You!" screeched the lady as Elizabeth stepped up to Darcy's side. "Is this the thanks I receive for my attention to you in March and April? I suppose I should have expected one such as you to betray me in this fashion, for your base nature reveals you."

"I know not of what betrayal you speak, Lady Catherine," replied Elizabeth, the coolness of her tone in direct contrast with Lady Catherine's fury. "There is no connection between us, such that I must bow to your whims. I stayed in Kent with my dear friend—a few invitations to dinner does not an obligation make."

"And what of your promise to refuse any overtures Darcy made? How do you defend yourself on that score?"

"I promised nothing," replied Elizabeth. "If you recall, I said nothing more than I could not imagine the end you suggested coming to pass."

"And yet, here you are," spat her ladyship.

Darcy turned uneasily. They had put the story out that their engagement was a longstanding one from Kent, and while he did not like the falsehood, it was necessary to protect Elizabeth's reputation. A wrong word here could undo everything they sought to gain.

But he need not have concerned himself, for Elizabeth was not so easily tripped up. "I shall not bandy words of how or when Mr. Darcy and I came together. The fault is yours for obsessing over such a ridiculous notion as to force *my husband* to marry your daughter!"

"It is not ridiculous!" thundered the lady. "You have upset the wishes of three families with your arts and allurements. Do you suppose I will fade away so easily when thwarted in such a manner?"

"It seems you have little choice."

Darcy was proud of his new wife; few possessed the internal resources to defy his aunt with such determination, yet here she was, responding to the lady's attacks with neither hesitation nor fear. Lady Catherine noticed it, for, in her fury, Darcy thought her ready to lash out, to release her frustration in a sudden burst of violence. But his cousin, Viscount Banbury, saw it too, and he stepped forward to restrain his aunt.

"That is enough, Aunt Catherine. It is time you depart, for you have disrupted this celebration enough."

"I have not even begun," spat Lady Catherine. Her eyes roamed around the room and fell on one, in particular. "And Georgiana, sitting there with girls not fit to be her maids! Are you caught in this madness too?"

"That is enough, Lady Catherine," growled Darcy. "You will not speak to my sister again."

"It is clear the Darcy blood has diluted the noble Fitzwilliam blood in you both." Lady Catherine regarded Darcy amid a storm of rage and contempt. "You think me so easily mastered, but you have not considered the means I have at my disposal to render you a pariah in all society. Do you suppose I will not use it with your treachery bared open?"

"Get out, Aunt Catherine," commanded Banbury. "You will gain nothing by following through with this mad design."

"I will expose the Darcy family for the brittle line they are! And I shall begin by doing so here and now."

"No, you will not!"

The authoritative voice interrupted their argument, and every eye swung to the newcomer, a tall, aristocratic man, bearing a close resemblance to his sons. The earl had come; Darcy had no notion of how he had arrived so quickly or how he knew where to go, but relief washed over him. Lord Matlock was the one man who could control his sister, the one person in the world she might obey. It saved Darcy from drastic action, for he had been about to throw his aunt over his shoulder and carry her from the room, bellowing all the way if needs must.

"Have you finally lost your senses, Catherine?" demanded the earl, stepping to his sister and forcing her to face him.

"Brother —" began she, but Lord Matlock would not allow her to continue.

"Not another word! You have disrupted this house long enough."

Lord Matlock turned in the general direction of the party and bowed to them. "Please accept my apologies for my sister's actions. We shall take our argument to the drive."

Then with a stern gesture that brooked no disobedience, he ushered his sister from the room. Lady Catherine was not willing, but she had always been reluctant to cross her brother, who she knew wielded great power. Thus, she stalked from Longbourn, holding her head high as if she were a queen. Exchanging a look with his cousins, Darcy followed them, determined not to be left out of the ensuing discussion.

But there was no discussion, for as soon as they gained the drive, the earl tore into his sister, dressing her down in a manner she would not soon forget. Darcy doubted anyone had spoken to her ladyship in such a way since she had been a child.

"Of all the low, disgusting, stupid things you could have done, Catherine, this is the most egregious! What were you thinking, barging into such a place where you know no one and speaking as if you were the wife of a fishmonger?"

"Blame Darcy!" cried she, jabbing one skeletal finger at him. "He forced me to this end. If he had only married my daughter as he ought, all would be well!"

"I have long known this delusion had a hold on your heart," said Lord Matlock. "But had I known it ruled you to this extent, I would have consigned you to Bedlam many years ago."

"You have not that power," said the lady, though a hint of fear showed in her eyes.

"Do not be foolish!" snapped his lordship. "The power, I most certainly have. All that would hold me back is the fear of revealing our family's weakness to society. Given your behavior, that may be a better end than allowing you to continue to act in your depraved way.

"Did you suppose I would stand by and allow you to ruin my niece without opposition? Do you consider me so ineffectual?"

"This does not concern—"

"Of course, it concerns me, daft woman!" roared the earl. "Georgiana is my niece—I would be a poor uncle, indeed, if I did not do my utmost to protect her. What foulness has invaded your mind?"

Lady Catherine, for once, held her tongue, though her face was a mass of taut muscles, veins striving against the confines of her skin. When Lord Matlock saw he had effectively silenced her, he nodded in grim satisfaction, his eyes finding Darcy.

"Might I assume the wedding has already taken place? Given what I just saw in that house, I cannot think otherwise."

"It has," replied Darcy. "And I am overjoyed with my choice."

His uncle nodded, though Darcy knew he would be the focus of his interrogation once they had disposed of Lady Catherine.

"Then there is nothing more you can do, Catherine. Even vengeance would serve you ill for much of that gossip would redound back on you, with Darcy's public repudiation of your claim of an engagement all these years. The only option left for you is to return to Rosings Park and manage your disappointment as best you can.

"Of Georgiana, you will breathe not a word, do you hear me?"

When Lady Catherine did not move a muscle, her brother stepped close to her and growled: "Do not test me, Catherine, for you will not like the result. I require verbal confirmation of your understanding and your commitment to remaining silent."

"Very well," said Lady Catherine. "But know this, Darcy: from this moment forward you are dead to me and mine. Your betrayal is the last act between us. Do not come to Rosings, for you will find my doors closed to you."

"If you do not recall, Aunt Catherine," replied Darcy, "I severed all connection between us when I left Kent. Even if I was inclined to relent, I shall not associate with one so lacking in common decency. You cannot sever what does not exist."

The lady's nostrils flared, but she said nothing further. Instead, she turned on her heel, stalked to her carriage, and soon the dust kicked up by the carriage wheels announced her departure. The four men remaining behind watched her depart.

"That woman will be the death of me," muttered Lord Matlock when the carriage left the drive.

"She will not affect me a jot," said Darcy. "I meant what I said, uncle; I will not associate with her again, nor will I even tolerate her company."

Lord Matlock turned to Darcy and regarded him. "I cannot blame you. If the option existed for me, I would not hesitate to take it. But I must endure her, for there is no other option."

A nod was all Darcy allowed himself, for there was little reason to further assert what he had already stated.

"I would ask you about this woman to whom you have tied yourself," continued his lordship after a moment. "Knowing you as I do, I hardly suspect you would offer for a woman who was a simpleton or a fortune hunter. And yet, by all accounts, she is not of your level of society."

Lord Matlock looked about and gestured to the estate. "It appears to be a good estate, and the man who owns it is a man of some conscience, for there is little amiss with his property that one can see. Yet, the size of the estate renders him a country gentleman or perhaps a squire, one with little societal prominence. If you did not wish to marry Anne, why did you not search for a woman more acceptable to society?"

Fitzwilliam opened his mouth to respond, but Darcy motioned him to silence. When he saw it, Lord Matlock nodded with approval. There would be time for Fitzwilliam to add his praise of Elizabeth later — for now it was best that Darcy answer his uncle's questions.

"Do you suppose I would choose a woman of society with alacrity when I have disparaged every new crop of debutantes since I entered society myself?"

The laughter Darcy provoked in his cousins accompanied Banbury's soft: "Aye, that is the rub!"

Even the earl appeared to appreciate the humor in Darcy's statement, though his steady look informed Darcy he had not yet received the answer he desired.

"I find Miss Elizabeth—or rather Mrs. Darcy now—suits me in every particular, Uncle. She is a gem among women, calm and poised, yet lively, beautiful, compassionate, and intelligent. While so many of my peers search for a wife to be a pretty bauble on their arms, I wish for more from a marriage. I believe I have found it in my new wife."

The earl regarded him for a long moment before he turned to Fitzwilliam. "As you were so eager to speak a moment ago, perhaps you wish to corroborate Darcy's account of his new wife? As I recall, you have known her longer than James has."

"I only met her this morning when I came for the wedding," supplied Banbury.

"I concur with Darcy," said Fitzwilliam. "Had I the means to keep a woman without a handsome dowry in any kind of comfort, I might have considered pursuing her myself."

"Well, that is high praise, indeed," said Lord Matlock. "And you know I would gladly provide for you, should you marry and leave the army."

"I do know it and I thank you," replied Fitzwilliam. "But the possibility did not exist anyway, not when I discerned Darcy's interest in her. You know I would never attempt to trod on his toes."

"Yes, I do," replied Lord Matlock. He turned back and studied Darcy. "Then this woman, though she is unknown in society and presumably lacks a season, will not embarrass us?"

"Perhaps you would like to take your own measure of her," suggested Darcy.

"I would like that very much," replied Lord Matlock. "But I should like your assessment before I do."

"Then I cannot give her a warm enough recommendation, Uncle," replied Darcy. "She will handle the ton with aplomb and will have all but the most recalcitrant eating from her palm in little time."

"She appeared to be quite capable to me, Father," said Banbury. Fitzwilliam kept his silence.

The earl nodded. "Then, I would like an introduction, Darcy. Shall we?"

Had Elizabeth not had the members of her local community to occupy her attention, she was afraid she would gain a true understanding of her mother's nerves to make her earlier awareness a pale imitation. Elizabeth was now bound to Mr. Darcy, and nothing short of an annulment would change that—in short, there was no going back. The earl had controlled his sister and removed her from the harm she was causing, but Elizabeth yet had no notion of the truth of his opinion. For all she was aware, he intended to silence his sister, but would withhold support from her union with Mr. Darcy. Such thoughts might have held sway if Elizabeth had not had to speak to her friends and neighbors to give them some explanation for the disruption that had appeared in their midst.

A welcome distraction it was. Elizabeth did not know how many times she had told the abbreviated story of Lady Catherine's obsession with a supposed engagement between her daughter and Mr. Darcy, but it seemed to have been more than a hundred. Most of those present understood her inference of the lady's confidence in her infallibility and recognized her assertion that Mr. Darcy had been well within his rights to choose his wife. Many were aware her story was incomplete, but no one called her on it, for they knew her and supported her, and they knew it was none of their concern.

The company was a subdued one while they waited for Mr. Darcy to return. That no one attempted to go to the front of the house and overhear what they were saying was a source of much relief. It may have been that no one wished to be the first to move in such a blatant attempt to eavesdrop, but whatever the reason, she could not but feel the gratitude of their forbearance.

"That was a bit of excitement, was it not, Lizzy?" asked Mr. Bennet as she was moving among the guests.

"I could do without your sardonic levity at present, Papa," replied she, in a tone *almost* free of pique.

"That much is clear," replied he, no hint of repentance staining his voice. "But I must thank you for it nonetheless, for it will keep me diverted for some time. Do not tell me you are so missish that you cannot withstand and laugh at a little absurdity."

"At an event so important as my wedding breakfast, I believe I could cheerfully do without such things."

"I dare say you could," replied her father, his grin never wavering.

Elizabeth could not help but laugh, rueful though it was. In several years, she believed she could look back on this day with lighter spirits. Now, however, it was the cruelest of punishments. What a reprehensible creature Lady Catherine was! If Elizabeth was never in her company again, she would be well pleased!

Then Sir William drew nearer, and Elizabeth's attention turned to him. The morose look he presented was far beyond what Elizabeth had ever seen in the usually jovial gentleman, such that she did not know what to make of him.

"First, I wish to offer my felicitations," said the gentleman, a hint of a smile lighting his face. "But then I fear I must also apologize."

"I have no notion for what," said Elizabeth, confused.

"Ah, but you have not heard my account, for I fear Lady Catherine's coming was my fault. For you see, I wrote to Charlotte about your upcoming nuptials. I can only surmise that Lady Catherine learned of it through her husband, for Charlotte would do nothing other than rejoice for you."

"Oh, Sir William," said Elizabeth, wondering that they had not thought to caution the one link anyone in the community had to Lady Catherine's domain, "please do not think about it for another moment. Perhaps events transpired as you suppose, but we did not speak of your need to keep it from your son-in-law. It never occurred to us."

"And Lady Catherine's assertions are without foundation, I suppose?"

The man was not questioning her; rather he was searching for a bit of comfort on that score. A man such as Sir William, who put much stock in civility and had experience with the higher classes, would worry about such things. He had never felt the effects before, but Sir William was aware of the power held by those such as Lady Catherine.

"According to my husband," said Elizabeth, her reference to Mr. Darcy in such terms deliberate, "the engagement of which Lady Catherine speaks was never mentioned by his mother and never sanctioned by his father."

"That is well, then," said Sir William, apparently relieved.

"If I am not mistaken," said Mr. Bennet, "Mr. Darcy will return soon. Shall we not allow Elizabeth to greet her new family in private?"

The jovial gentleman returned, and he nodded, offering his congratulations again, before following Bennet away. How her father knew, Elizabeth could not say, but a moment later Mr. Darcy entered the room, leading his uncle and cousins. When he caught sight of her, he allowed a brilliant smile and approached her, reaching forward to clasp her hands.

"Lady Catherine is gone," said he in a low tone meant for her ears alone. "And my uncle wishes to make your acquaintance."

Sensible as she was to the effect this would have on her neighbors Elizabeth could feel nothing but gratitude for the earl's gesture. When he stepped forward, Mr. Darcy performed the introductions, and she responded with a low curtsey, feeling the eyes of everyone in the company on her form.

"Mrs. Darcy," said the earl, his tone gracious, "allow me to welcome you to the family. I am delighted to make your acquaintance, and my wife—who felt unequal to another journey north after our long sojourn from Ireland—is very much desirous of knowing you too."

A sigh seemed to pass through the assembled as if they had waited for the approbation of Mr. Darcy's relations before they would allow themselves to relax. Elizabeth did not give them another moment's thought, for all her focus was on the tall and powerful man before her.

"I thank you, your lordship," said she, rising again to stand erect before him. "I feel all the privilege of your welcome, for it is my understanding there are certain elements of society who may not approve."

The earl laughed at her impertinent remark, and Colonel Fitzwilliam leaned forward and said *sotto voce*: "I told you that you would find her delightful, Father."

"Indeed, you did, Son," said the earl, still chuckling. He fixed Elizabeth with an appraising look. "Not all of my station are the same as my sister, who has ever been difficult to endure. Given what I have seen from you in only a moment, I suspect you will charm them with your wit, and handle naysayers with the greatest aplomb."

"I shall do my best, my lord," replied Elizabeth. "With Mr. Darcy's support, I feel confident enough to face them all."

"And we shall bear you up as well." Then he fixed her with sternness and added: "But you are my niece, and I would not have you address me so formally. Darcy is much too stodgy to call me Uncle Hugh, but I should be delighted if you would favor me so."

"Uncle Hugh it is," agreed Elizabeth.

They stood about for several moments speaking, and then when the earl mentioned his desire to be introduced to her parents, Elizabeth complied. Mrs. Bennet, she noted, was quite in awe of hosting an earl in her home, and she remained silent, while Elizabeth's sisters were scarcely less amazed. Mr. Bennet, however, made a jest, and within moments they were speaking together with much more animation than Elizabeth might have expected. Throughout the rest of the breakfast, Elizabeth noted that the earl allowed himself to be introduced to many in the company, and few showed any less deference than Mrs. Bennet.

As for Elizabeth's neighbors and friends, it appeared the welcome of an earl was good enough for them. The congratulations that had subsided in the wake of Lady Catherine's coming renewed tenfold, rendering Elizabeth grateful for her new uncle's calculated actions. The Bennets, she knew, would soon be lauded as the most fortunate family in the vicinity, with their new connection to the nobility. It was a matter to be discussed at length in the sitting-rooms of the neighborhood denizens, but it would now be a matter of amazement rather than gossip.

"Ah, Lizzy," said her Aunt Gardiner as she approached. "I had wondered when Mr. Darcy first came to my home whether he had some other motivation for his civility."

"As I recall," said Elizabeth. "It appears you were correct."

"I was. I hope you will forgive me my unseemly satisfaction."

Aunt Gardiner gathered Elizabeth in for an embrace and said in a low tone: "As I recall, you did not precisely welcome my conjecture. Are you happy, Lizzy?"

"I hardly know at present," replied Elizabeth. "What I can say is that I am not unhappy; I suspect bliss may be on the horizon, but it is early to tell."

"That is welcome intelligence," replied she. "You are a sensible girl. If you only allow yourself to remain open to the possibility, I suspect you will do well."

"Ah, Lizzy," said Uncle Gardiner, joining them with a grin. "It appears you are due all congratulations. I like your new husband very much."

"He is an excellent man, Uncle," said Elizabeth, feeling every bit of the truth of her words.

"I dare say he is. But now we have a dilemma, for we meant to offer to take you on our tour of the north this summer. As you are already married, we shall need to find another traveling companion."

"If you do not recall, I invited you to stay at Pemberley."

Mr. Darcy strode up with a look of welcome for Elizabeth's aunt and uncle. "And as my wife's family is to come also, we can make a party of it."

Mrs. Gardiner turned a speculative look on Elizabeth. "Your family is to come?"

"They are, Aunt," said Elizabeth. "Mr. Darcy and I would be pleased if you also accepted the invitation."

"We already have," said Uncle Gardiner. "But I had not known your family was also to join us." He turned and grin at Mr. Darcy. "You should prepare for a horde to descend on your halls, sir. The grand old place may never be the same!"

"Pemberley has been quiet too long, Mr. Gardiner. I hope in the coming years it will once again ring with the happiness of its occupants."

The Gardiners laughed and Mrs. Gardiner exclaimed: "Then you had best begin at once, sir. Elizabeth comes from strong stock, as evidenced by her mother. I am certain she will be pleased to repopulate the Darcy family to its greatest extent!"

To the amusement of them all, Elizabeth felt her cheeks heating and could not help the glare she directed at them. They were too merry a party to do anything other than laugh at her faux outrage, the conversation continuing in animation among them, the subject of the coming summer and the timing of their gathering.

And as she stood amid those she loved, listening to their banter, Elizabeth realized she had come to esteem Mr. Darcy. She esteemed him very much. It was not, perhaps, the deep love she had expected to feel for her husband, but she knew one good push would be all it would take to bring her to that state of ecstasy. Elizabeth could hardly wait.

CHAPTER XV

" *E*lizabeth! I have been searching for you, for I have a bit of news you will no doubt find as diverting as I have."

Looking up from her book, Elizabeth smiled at her husband, enough invitation for him to join her on the settee. She supposed he might have thought to look for her in her private sitting-room, for she often retreated there when the company at Pemberley became too much. Then again, William knew her well enough by now to know her ways, for three months of marriage had taught each much of the other.

At present, he looked very handsome, indeed, his boyish grin radiating a charm Elizabeth had never thought the dour Mr. Darcy possessed. That Mr. Darcy had proven as false and fleeting as the one who looked at her now had become her cherished image of her husband. He was not a perfect man by any means, and he often tended toward brooding. But Elizabeth had determined to laugh him out of it whenever he descended to such depths, and in this, she seemed to attain more success the more she attempted it.

"And what is this news?" asked she.

"It is of my cousin Anne de Bourgh and, more particularly, of her mother."

Mr. Darcy brandished the letter he held in his hands, the existence of which Elizabeth had not noted as she had considered her husband. The barely concealed hilarity was enough to stimulate her interest, for Mr. Darcy was rarely of a disposition to give into much overt mirth.

"You see," said he, "it appears my aunt has finally gone too far. After ranting and raving about our union for some time, she fell to brooding and then to plotting. When she arranged for Anne to meet several eligible gentlemen, all of the nobility, intending to show us all that she could find a more illustrious marriage for her daughter, Anne's patience snapped."

Elizabeth grinned. "And it could not happen to a more deserving recipient. What did she do?"

"Anne wrote to our uncle, and he descended on Rosings in fire and fury, dressed Lady Catherine down yet again, and threw all the pretenders from the house." Mr. Darcy laughed delightedly as he looked down at the letter, scanning its contents. "Then he installed Anne as the mistress of the estate and forced Lady Catherine to the dower house."

"That *is* a surprise," said Elizabeth. "Given what I know of your cousin, I might not have thought she had the fortitude to defy her mother."

"You are not the only one," replied William. "Fitzwilliam is as flummoxed by these events as I am myself. Anne has decreed that her mother will not enter Rosings again until she has made an apology to them all, and it appears Lady Catherine has obeyed her edict!"

"What a wonderful thought," said Elizabeth with a smirk. "To be honest, I care not if Lady Catherine ever offers an apology. But her present straits appear to be nothing less than poetic justice, and I cannot but reflect on how much she deserves it."

"You will receive no disagreement from me," replied William.

Elizabeth regarded him for a long moment and said: "I suppose you have no word of how Mr. Collins is taking his patroness's demotion? He worships the very ground upon which she walks."

"After our wedding, as you know, Lady Catherine descended on the parsonage and assaulted him for allowing his wife to invite you to Hunsford. I suspect his feelings of awe for Lady Catherine have cooled substantially since then."

"Perhaps you are correct. Then he will latch onto your cousin as his new excellent patroness."

Mr. Darcy gave her a smirk. "And he will find little purchase there. Anne will not manage him to the extent that her mother did. I suspect she will wish to have little to do with him."

"For that, I can only be grateful," replied Elizabeth. "For Charlotte's sake, you understand. It cannot be comfortable to live with one's husband and know another is the mistress of his home."

"No, I cannot suppose it is." Mr. Darcy turned a grin on her. "It seems your mother has finally realized you will not act as she wishes. I have not heard her speak of the necessity of redecorating the front sitting-room in several days now."

Elizabeth shook her head with exasperation. Mrs. Bennet had definite ideas about the desirability for newly married ladies to put their stamp on their husband's home. Elizabeth was ready and willing to redecorate any chambers that required it, and she had several thoughts in mind for the improvement of the room she currently occupied. But she would not act on nothing more than the desire to prove she was the mistress and her mother's insistence.

"There is no need to do anything at present with that room," said she. "It is very fine already and in need of nothing."

"And yet you know you may do what you wish when you wish it."

With a fond smile, Elizabeth nodded. "I am aware of it. But there is little reason for expenditures for vanity's sake alone. My mother has never had much ability to control me. She does not like it, but she wishes to be invited to Pemberley again, so she will not push further."

William gave her a quizzical look. "Did something pass between you of which I am not aware?"

"No," replied Elizabeth. "But my mother and I understand each other, at least to that extent. My mother does not comprehend my independence, but she has a healthy respect for it."

The nod with which her husband responded was no less than distracted. "Bingley has watched what unfolded between you with astonishment. He will not renew the lease on Netherfield, for he fears your mother will turn her attention upon Jane."

Elizabeth could not help but roll her eyes. "Yes, and Mother believes Jane is less capable of withstanding her than I, though she misjudges my sister. Jane can be as immovable as a boulder if she feels she is in the right. Do you suppose Mr. Bingley will begin looking for an estate at once?"

"He has already approached me on the subject," replied Mr. Darcy, his grin showing his delight. "Bingley has taken his sister's good advice, has decided Derbyshire is the best of all counties and will purchase as close to Pemberley as possible."

Delight surged through Elizabeth's breast, and she clapped her hands. "That is excellent news! One drawback to marriage to you was the distance I would be from Jane. Now that she is to live here, my happiness could not be more complete!"

"I knew you would enjoy it," said William. "But I am surprised your sister did not tell you."

"Oh, it is some mischievousness on Jane's part. But I shall have my vengeance on her."

"Bingley can hardly wait for the wedding. I suspect he is envious of our felicity."

"He will soon have his own. It is less than a month to his nuptials."

"And we must return to Hertfordshire." William regarded her with interest. "Do you anticipate returning to the place of your birth, where my aunt so thoroughly disrupted our wedding breakfast?"

"There is no impediment, I should think," replied Elizabeth. "From what my father has informed me, the gossip prevalent in the neighborhood concerned Lady Catherine's utter lack of restraint. I should think *you* would be in greater danger from a return than I."

"If you do not consider my position in life," said Mr. Darcy, effecting a haughty look of disdain. "I *am* the scion of an earl, the man they would not like to offend. I think I shall be quite safe among your neighbors."

"You do that so well!" exclaimed Elizabeth amid her mirth. "If I did not now know you better, I might have thought that haughty Darcy disdain was as real as I did when we first met."

"Ah, but it *is* real," replied he, enjoying their banter. "There are many in London who can attest to it."

"But they do not know you as well as I do," said Elizabeth. Then she paused and considered other matters. "I hope the sudden loudness of the house does not cause you to repine the invitation that brought all my family here. Aunt's children are well behaved, but even they must run at times, and Kitty and Lydia are perhaps the loudest of them all!"

"Nothing of the sort," replied William. "As I informed your aunt and uncle, there is a life in Pemberley that has not existed here for many years. And if it becomes too much, there is a stout door between my study and the rest of the house!

"As there is between this sitting-room and the outside world," agreed Elizabeth.

"Besides," continued William, "I hope that someday we will have our own children to fill the halls of our home."

"I hope you do not expect to fill *all* the halls, sir," replied Elizabeth. "This is a *very* large house."

"Well, we shall simply need to do our best."

They fell into companionable silence thereafter, Elizabeth caught up in her reminiscences, her continued astonishment for her position here in this house, in her husband's life, and this after she had, only a few months before, considered him a proud and conceited man! What changes had come over her!

For his part, William stayed beside her, the letter forgotten on the table before them, one hand playing with an errant lock escaped from her coiffure. He had often commented on her hair, that unruly mass of dark curls Elizabeth had despaired of since she had been a girl. William was always running his fingers through it, speaking of its soft silkiness. More than once he had undone the efforts of her maid in the middle of the day, no less!

At present, however, he did not seem to concentrate on it as he often did. Rather, he was looking at nothing, a faint sense of absorption in something only he could see. It was often thus with William, for even as she had come to know him, had seen he was not always the taciturn man she had thought him to be, he often bent his mind to reflection. It was one of his more endearing traits.

"You spoke of drawbacks to marrying me," said William suddenly a few moments later. "Are there others?"

Elizabeth instinctively caught the meaning in his question, though for the moment she held back her grin. "At the time, there were several, if you recall."

"And do they still concern you?" asked he, his eyes searching her as if the truth was hidden in their depths. Perhaps it was.

"Not a one that I can think of," replied Elizabeth.

He regarded her as if uncertain of her meaning. Giving him a loving smile, Elizabeth cupped his cheek in her hand and leaned in to kiss him. It was an action she had rarely initiated with him, though she had learned to enjoy their intimacy very much.

"Silly man," murmured she against his lips. "There is nowhere I would rather be than here with you for a lifetime. I love you. It has taken me some time to realize it, but I have found what I felt I was missing. Do not suppose I shall ever regret our union, for I shall not."

Elizabeth paused and grinned. "Then again, perhaps there were some things to regret, including your unfortunate relation. But we have relegated her to the past, so I shall not give her a jot more of my concern!"

"That is excellent, Elizabeth," replied Mr. Darcy, leaning in for more. "And just so we are even, I am so much in love with you that my heart might burst."

Even if Elizabeth had possessed coherent thought enough to reply, his ministrations distracted her. Willing to be distracted, she sighed and drew him closer. Against all her expectations, beyond any imagination, she was now home. She could not be happier.

The End

MORE GREAT TITLES FROM
ONE GOOD SONNET PUBLISHING!

PRIDE AND PREJUDICE VARIATIONS

By Jann Rowland

Acting on Faith
A Life from the Ashes (Sequel to
Acting on Faith)
Open Your Eyes
Implacable Resentment
An Unlikely Friendship
Bound by Love
Cassandra
Obsession
Shadows Over Longbourn
The Mistress of Longbourn
My Brother's Keeper
Coincidence
The Angel of Longbourn
Chaos Comes to Kent
In the Wilds of Derbyshire
The Companion
Out of Obscurity
What Comes Between Cousins
A Tale of Two Courtships
Murder at Netherfield
Whispers of the Heart
A Gift for Elizabeth
Mr. Bennet Takes Charge

The Impulse of the Moment
The Challenge of Entail
A Matchmaking Mother
Another Proposal
With Love's Light Wings
Flight to Gretna Green
Mrs. Bennet's Favorite Daughter
Her Indomitable Resolve
Love and Libertine
In Default of Heirs Male
Among Intimate Acquaintances
Danger at the Netherfield Ball
More Agreeably Engaged
Unintended Consequences

By Lelia Eye

Netherfield's Secret
A Sister's Sacrifice

By Colin Rowland

The Parson's Rescue
Hidden Desires
Disgraceful Conduct

PRIDE AND PREJUDICE SERIES

By Jann Rowland

COURAGE ALWAYS RISES: THE BENNET SAGA

The Heir's Disgrace
Volume II Untitled*
Volume III Untitled*

NO CAUSE TO REPINE

A Tacit Engagement
Scandalous Falsehoods
Upstart Pretensions
Quitting the Sphere
No Cause to Repine Box Set

BONDS OF LIFE

Bonds of Friendship
Bonds of Love

* Forthcoming

OTHER GENRES BY
ONE GOOD SONNET PUBLISHING

FANTASY

By Jann Rowland & Lelia Eye

EARTH AND SKY SERIES

On Wings of Air
On Lonely Paths
On Tides of Fate*

FAIRYTALE

By Lelia Eye

The Princes and the Peas: A Tale of Robin Hood

SMOTHERED ROSE TRILOGY

Thorny
Unsoiled
Roseblood

* Forthcoming

About the Author

Jann Rowland

Jann Rowland is a Canadian, born and bred. Other than a two-year span in which he lived in Japan, he has been a resident of the Great White North his entire life, though he professes to still hate the winters.

Though Jann did not start writing until his mid-twenties, writing has grown from a hobby to an all-consuming passion. His interests as a child were almost exclusively centered on the exotic fantasy worlds of Tolkien and Eddings, among a host of others. As an adult, his interests have grown to include historical fiction and romance, with a particular focus on the works of Jane Austen.

When Jann is not writing, he enjoys rooting for his favorite sports teams. He is also a master musician (in his own mind) who enjoys playing piano and singing as well as moonlighting as the choir director in his church's congregation.

Jann lives in Alberta with his wife of more than twenty years, two grown sons, and one young daughter. He is convinced that whatever hair he has left will be entirely gone by the time his little girl hits her teenage years. Sadly, though he has told his daughter repeatedly that she is not allowed to grow up, she continues to ignore him.

Please let him know what you think or sign up for their mailing list to learn about future publications:

Website:	http://onegoodsonnet.com/
Facebook:	https://facebook.com/OneGoodSonnetPublishing/
Twitter:	**@OneGoodSonnet**
Mailing List:	http://eepurl.com/bol2p9

Made in the USA
Las Vegas, NV
30 June 2022

50926736R00100